I Married a Psychic

Marv Lincoln

Book 1: The Vortex Conspiracy

Thunder Mountain Productions

I MARRIED A PSYCHIC
Book 1: The Vortex Conspiracy
Copyright © 2007 by Marvin H. Lincoln.

A Thunder Mountain Productions book
Printed in the United States of America

Cover illustration © 2007 by Pamela Becker
Book design by Anugito Ten Voorde, Artline Graphics
Photo credit: Back cover and Log On:
Photos by DheeLight, dheelight@earthlink.net

ISBN 978-09799208-0-6
Library of Congress Control Number: 2007906493

Thunder Mountain Productions
P.O. Box 3804
Sedona, AZ 86340

Contact information:
www.Vortex23.com (sales and marketing)
marv@vortex23.com

www.PamelaBeckerCreations.com (cover artist)

Dedication

This book is dedicated to my two muses:

Liberty Lincoln, my beloved wife and life partner,

and Maggie Lincoln, my devoted pussycat.

Without their help, inspiration, love, and support,

this book would not have been possible.

Log On   ≫   ≫   ≫

Confessions of a Sci-Fi Fanatic

Ever since I have been able to read beyond the level of "Fun with Dick and Jane" and Dr. Seuss, I have been a fanatic reader of science fiction.

I cut my baby teeth on Ray Bradbury and Arthur C. Clarke, then dived headlong into the strange, alternate worlds created by such masters of the craft as Heinlein, Asimov, A.E. Van Vogt, Frederick Pohl, Larry Niven, Poul Anderson, Anne McCaffrey, Ursula K. Le Guin. And many, many more.

Of course Vonnegut and Huxley and Philip K. Dick are high on my list. Ruling the pantheon today are my favorite cyberpunk, William Gibson, and his cyberbuddy Bruce Sterling, perhaps today's most influential sci-fi authors.

I have been a Trekkie since Star Trek I in 1966, and after the brilliant Star Trek TNG, I lost interest in the sequels. In the distant past, I wrote and sold several sci-fi short stories to special interest magazines. (My favorite, "The University," was a brazen knock-off of Huxley's "Brave New World.")

Thus my street cred in science fiction.

"I Married a Psychic" is my first novel in the genre. But now S-F comes under the umbrella of a relatively new and exciting genre called Visionary Fiction. The website VisionaryFiction.org describes it as "fiction in which the expansion of the human mind drives the plot."

The genre covers everything from novels like this one, containing elements of psychic and paranormal experience, to Carlos Castaneda's "The Teachings Of Don Juan" to the Harry Potter books to works of fantasy and even religion. Personally, I am happy to have this book included in the new genre of Visionary Fiction, and to join the luminaries already in the fold! Thank you, Vi-Fi overlords.

Creating this book has been an exhilarating experience, a wild ride full of surprise and amazing twists and turns. It is probably a cliché by now to say that the book came "through me," but it did, especially when I got out of my own way and just let the words and ideas flow onto the blank screen of my iMac G5 monitor. This was not channeled material; the novel no doubt arose from my subconscious mind and from real-time recycling of memories.

My wife-muse-editor Liberty, a hopeless romantic, insists that the book is a so-called *roman à clef*. This is a French term for a novel in which real people or events appear with invented names; or, a story that depicts real people (usually famous, and often the author) under the guise of fiction. Often scandalous behavior is depicted. A *roman à clef* usually includes clues to the characters' true identities.

Recent *romans à clef* that come to mind are "The Devil Wears Prada;" "The Bell Jar," by and about Sylvia Plath; Kerouac's "On the Road;" "Postcards from the Edge" by Carrie Fisher; Hemingway's "The Sun Also Rises;" and "Tender Is the Night" by F. Scott Fitzgerald.

It is true that the lead characters in "I Married a Psychic" are loosely based on my wife and myself—after all, she *is* a psychic and I married her—and the events depicted herein are loosely based on real events, up to a point, although said events have been revised, modified and exaggerated for story and plot value. And to protect the innocent as well as the guilty.

But it might be difficult to place a sci-fi (or Visionary

5

Fiction, if you will) story into the *roman à clef* category. Unless Valentine Michael Smith, the alien from Mars in "Stranger in a Strange Land," represents Heinlein's alter ego, as one example. Or perhaps Phil Dick's characters were actually playing out the psychodrama of his life, although in an unworldly, paranoid setting. All writers of fiction write about what we know.

This book shifts back and forth in time, from the real or imagined past, which gradually meets the present, or the here and now in the book, where such events as traveling through transdimensional portals and remote viewing and teleportation and telekinesis are not unusual. So you have to pay attention.

In conclusion, let's just say that this book *might be based on real people* who met and fell in love and changed the world for the better through a series of improbable but perfectly reasonable events. It's visionary fiction, it's a love story, it's a wild adventure, and "I Married a Psychic" goes where no book has gone before. We guarantee it.

Marv Lincoln
Sedona, Arizona
September 2007

6

PART I

CHAPTER ONE

The Gathering Storm

Sedona
Present Day

Many call it Paradise. But in the high desert summer, when the clouds abandon us and the thermometer seems stuck at 100+ degrees day after day after day, and the heat seems determined to kill us all, there can be only one word to describe Sedona, Arizona:
Hell.

Shocking, isn't it, that such a beautiful place, home of stunning red rock formations and pure air and mysterious energies and fall colors in October and snow on the ground in December, could host such a flesh-roasting summer climate.

It's now late June, and the temperature has soared over 100 for several straight days. Every year now, it seems, is the hottest year on record. Scoffers? Doubters? Global warming is a vast left wing conspiracy, you say? Come to

Sedona in June. Step out of the air conditioning for 10 minutes. Or better yet, linger in Phoenix for the full complement of punishment.

And so it is that I hunker down in my air-conditioned Sedona home, waiting until hell freezes over, frightened—yes, frightened—to venture outside to the mailbox. For one thing, the temperature is now at 108, a new record for this date. Such temperatures have been known to destroy brain cells by the millions, and I can't afford to lose any.

Or maybe I'm just a wimp and can't handle what native Arizonans blithely call "dry heat." I'm not from around here.

Another reason I am hunkered down: I am afraid of what I will find in my mailbox. See Item 1, below. Furthermore, I have not even checked my e-mail for three days. See Items 1 and 3.

Me? I'm Marty Powers. I'm a forty-something writer, troublemaker and proprietor of a website called SedonaConfidential.com. I am married to a psychic named Leela.

I admit that I've got some serious problems right now. Here they are, not in order of importance or degree of peril:

1. My popular but controversial website has been causing a shitstorm in this little town. I've been stepping on some pretty big toes with my exposés of local corruption and scandals. A few days ago I found a dead rattlesnake in my mailbox. Hate messages flood my e-mail.

2. My wife probably knows that I've been shagging one of her best friends. It's hard to fool a psychic, much less your average, intuition-infused female.

3. My best male friend hacked the main (secure)

website of Homeland Security last week, and posted fake nude photos of a controversial female columnist on the home page. As a prank. Now the FBI is looking for the perpetrator and anyone who is known to hang out with said perpetrator.

So for me the heat is on. Indeed.

In Sedona, as in most of Arizona, the only thing that saves us from the grinding, soul-ripping heat is the Monsoon. This means the summer rainy season, and it nearly always arrives on the same day: July 7.

Actually, our Monsoon is pretty skimpy by Asian standards. In places like India it can rain for days on end and cause terrible flooding and wipe out whole villages. I have spent time in India. I know serious rain; I have had relationships with mildew. Still, our humble Arizona Monsoon is the safety valve that keeps many of us sane in the brutal Sedona summer.

We are beggars here. We wait for it, half mad, dry as a cactus. We beg, we pray, we make deals with God, we sacrifice our children for rain. We wait for that sign from above, the awesome first thunderclap, the signal that late afternoon showers are on the way. Our salvation. Rain o'er me, o gods of moisture!

By the end of June, I keep hearing that mumble of thunder many miles away. The gathering storm. Or maybe it's just something stirring deep in my root chakra.

So this is my situation in the here and now: Dark clouds hovering on the horizon. A damp gloom surrounding the red rocks. A nameless dread. Lurking rednecks, federal agents, cuckolded wives, dangerous friends. The storm approaches.

CHAPTER TWO

The Meeting

India
1985

It was the mid-Eighties and I was a nearly total burnout, looking for the meaning of life and for some relief from my existential angst. I also suffered from a terminal case of writer's block and my cocaine-and-booze habit was not working anymore.

So I renewed my passport and headed for India and wandered around for a few months. I met my wife-to-be at an ashram not far from Bombay—one of those post-Esalen experiments in higher consciousness and free love that seemed to deliver on the failed promises of the late Sixties.

Beautiful people from all over the world gathered at this ashram, thousands of seekers. I had never seen so many beautiful women, all shiny-eyed and available, excited and giggling at nothing, speaking in tongues or perhaps that was just Portuguese or Italian or Low German or Japanese.

The guru, a bearded mystic who looked like you would imagine God Himself to look, was some kind of super-genius who wore simple white robes and emanated a kind of divine energy. Every morning at discourse he offered his enraptured audience a heady stew of Zen, Wilhelm Reich, Nietzsche, Buddha, Eastern religion and Western pop psychology, plus jokes designed to offend every race, creed and religion.

Some days he would answer questions sent in by people. I decided to throw him a curve. He swung at it. "What is the meaning of life?" I asked.

He started off gently. "Life has no meaning, except for life itself," he said. "Life is the only truth there is. So rejoice! Dance, sing, enjoy. No need to be serious. It is a cosmic joke."

Then, seeing through the frivolity of my question and my inherent trickiness, he proceeded to tear me a new one from the podium. I cringed silently as he ripped my ego to shreds for 20 minutes, then finished with, "But there is still hope for you. Just meditate. And do a few groups."

This ashram was very big on group therapy, and I figured I needed to clear out a few cobwebs so I did every encounter group they offered. Somehow I survived.

For dessert, I signed up for the Tantra group. Tantra is an ancient spiritual practice, often misunderstood. The word literally means "expansion of consciousness." It also means total acceptance of everything, no matter what happens. No complaining. What is, is.

But to most people in the modern world, Tantra means sex energy. That's what this Tantra group was all about—exploring sex in all its forms, with awareness, but also with totality. At this ashram, totality was a key word. So during the five-day group, everything was OK: group sex, homo sex, rape and bondage fantasies, straight sex, kinky sex. Just nothing forced or too out there.

On opening day I saw her walking into the group room, wearing a long, flowing maroon robe, dark hair around her shoulders, flashing green eyes; a goddess. She was from California; we had at least one thing in common, both from L.A., which I learned the first morning. She would look me straight in the eyes for several seconds, then look away, a flirt, a coquette, a tantalizing tease.

I picked her as my partner for the afternoon exercise, which was the classic Tantric Sex Ritual. She said yes. Goddess and god, energies merging, rising higher in consciousness together. Naked. Woman faces man, riding his thighs, they meditate for…half an hour? I was slowly dying. This was taking too long. I was hungry.

Earlier she had said her name was Leela, her spiritual name. Leela means "divine play" in Sanskrit. Her real name was LeAnn; I preferred Leela. Her voice was velvet. She had the body of a dancer, lean and lithe and firm, long slender legs, surprisingly ample buttocks and breasts. Add to this a beautiful, heart-shaped face and high, bold cheekbones. The whole package added up to one word: dreamgirl. On the physical plane, anyway.

We had spoken about 30 words together during our ritual, and meditated together for what seemed like hours, when I entered her. She was wet and ready, breathing deeply. The idea of the Tantric ritual is that you don't hump and writhe and moan and then shoot off and go to the stars like in regular sex.

No. This is sacred sex. In Tantra, you don't move. For a long, long time. You just stay joined and become as one, with closed eyes. Deep in meditation. In Tantra, when the orgasm starts to arrive, it begins somewhere way out at sea. Then comes wave upon wave of cool energy. And then...

We came together. It was silent. It was amazing. Our simultaneous orgasm seemed to last forever, transcending space/time. Then it was over. We parted silently. First day of the Tantra group, finished. I saw Leela again and again in the next four days. We didn't speak, she wouldn't look at me. I watched her having sex with other guys, with other women, in a group, by herself during the masturbation exercise.

It made me crazy to watch her, but I kept busy too: a young beauty from Israel wanted some rough sex with a stranger; no problem. I did some mild bondage and hot sex with a dark-eyed fat girl from Rome, a threesome with two German women, straight sex with a couple of others, and the rest is lost in a lust-saturated haze.

After the group finished, I approached Leela and asked if I could see her in Los Angeles. She looked away. "I'm married," she said simply in a hushed voice, bordering on shame. She said she was leaving India the following morning.

"Oh," was all I could muster. My guts ached. Either I was totally smitten with this elusive goddess, or I had amoebic dysentery. Smitten I was, no doubt about it.

When I left the ashram several days later, I felt different, elevated in consciousness, a new man. The therapy groups had wrought some major changes, had pierced my armor. The Tantra group especially, while seeming to be about sex, worked on deeper levels. And I had learned some keys to meditation during my India adventure.

Change was in the air. I would never be the same. For one thing, I thought I knew who I was.

CHAPTER THREE

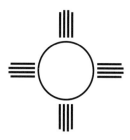

Trouble in Red Rock City

Sedona
Present Day

A knock at the front door—an ominous knock, the kind the cops usually employ to get your attention. I had kept my front door locked for days, an unusual practice for Sedona.

It's my friend Hacker aka John Hack. He doesn't usually knock because the door is never locked. Except now.

"Hot," he mutters as he brushes by me.

"No shit."

"Hottest summer on record, they say. Seems like every summer is the hottest summer on record."

"No shit. Whadda ya want, Hacker? You know I'm hunkered down here in my bunker, waiting for Armageddon."

He sprawls all over my couch, propping his size 12's on our secondhand coffee table. "Listen, Marty, you got

19

nothin to worry about. That piece in your website about local bigwigs hiring illegal immigrants—that'll blow over quick. Is that what's troubling you, Bunky?"

"You ever find a dead rattlesnake in your mailbox, dude?" I ask.

"Not lately. If I ever did, I'd track down the bastard who did it and strangle his scrawny red neck with it."

Hacker is always threatening to commit acts of violence on evil perpetrators, although he never does. My best friend is tall and muscular and built like Peyton Manning. He actually did play quarterback for UCLA back in the day. He is a dangerous man, but not in the ways you might imagine.

Hacker designed my website, Sedona Confidential, and serves as its webmaster. He is also, of course, a first-class hacker—thus the nickname—and he loves to hack the websites of politicians, celebrities, pretentious locals and of course government agencies.

He does this only for the prank value, and never drops viruses or worms on people. He says he is a legend in the global hacker community and won't tell even me his online handle, although he otherwise shares his most intimate secrets with me.

In Los Angeles, John Hack was a Unix programmer for one of the major aerospace companies. He doesn't like to talk about this chapter of his life story; apparently he was involved in some top-secret military stuff and this gnawed at his conscience for years. When the Internet became a reality in the early Nineties, Hacker learned how to write code in HTML and taught himself how to design websites.

In Sedona he is very well connected and is always giving me hot tips for stories on my website. Sometimes I

20

wonder if he has planted bugs in some very high places in this town, in bedrooms and boardrooms. This would explain how SedonaConfidential.com is able to publish some outrageous exposés.

My favorite column on the site, "Sedona Scandals," has caused quite a stir in Red Rock Country, revealing such things as government corruption, politicians with seriously vested interests, and more personal issues. This column is also why I am presently hunkered down waiting for the other shoe to drop.

"What about that babe you been ballin—does Leela know about her yet?"

"Probably." Leela, my beloved wife and soulmate, is presently in Flagstaff for a few days at a conference of psychics. She claims to be not only psychic but also clairvoyant, super-intuitive, telepathic, and a seer of secrets, so how could she not know?

The babe in question is one Alexis Adelstein (aka Aura Eaglefeather), and the alleged affair was a three-time infraction which took place in 1) her hospital bed; 2) the back of her van; and 3) our home, on the very couch on which Hacker now sprawls.

Aura is a local New Age type, an occasional psychic reader at the Crystal Palace and a part-time waitress. She is also a good friend of my wife's, and whenever they talk on the phone now my heart chakra slips up into my throat chakra. For the record, this is only the second or third time that I have cheated on my wife, not counting the times when we were separated for several months.

More on Aura later. In the moment, I am also concerned about Hacker's latest prank on the Homeland Security website.

21

"No problemo, Señor," he reassures in his deep voice. "They'll never trace it to you. Or me. I routed the lady's picture through a site in Slovenia, and then through a site used by the Sedona Planning & Zoning Commision for RFPs."

"Omigod." I swallow hard. "Hey, the feds have gotta know that we hang out together, and that you designed my site, and— and— and what the hell is an RFP?"

"Request for Proposal. Oh, yeah, I also did a little hack on the main White House site the other day. Forgot to tell ya. If you just type in whitehouse.gov, you will go immediately to this really nasty porno site from Russia. And—"

My cell phone is ringing. "Excuse me, convict Hack, it's my cell. Oh, it's only my wife." I am, of course, being sarcastic.

That sweet, familiar voice. "Hi, darling. How's the weather down there? It's a cool 80 in Flag right now."

I cover the mouthpiece and whisper to Hacker. "It's Leela. I'm sure she's calling to tell me she knows about Aura. You listen." I put the phone on speaker.

"It's about 109 here, dear, Fahrenheit, and my brains are about to fry. It's supposed to rain in a few days. Thirty percent chance. When are you coming home?" I try to keep my voice steady; my guts are churning.

"Marty, I need you to do me a favor. Aura called." (I am choking on my own saliva now.) "She's had a relapse and she's back in the hospital. I sense that she needs a friend right now, real bad. Y'know, I'm giving the keynote speech at tomorrow night's session here, so I can't come down. Would you just call her up and maybe you and Hacker could pay her a little visit?"

Was this some kind of code? Leela talked in code

sometimes, a code mainly understood by women. Maybe she knew about my transgression and was sparing me until she got back to Sedona.

A few weeks ago Aura had either been struck by lightning during a freak April thunderstorm or her body had been invaded and taken over by an alien consciousness from another dimension, I'm not sure which. She landed in the hospital from the incident, and that's where the trouble started. In her hospital bed. At Cottonwood General Hospital.

"Okay, sweetheart. Me and Hacker will pay her a visit. Maybe tomorrow."

"You okay, Marty? You sound stressed. What's going on there? Any more strangeness happen, any more rattlesnakes in our mailbox…?"

"It's the weather," I half-lie. "You know how the pressure builds up until it rains. My head feels like it's ready to explode."

"Take it easy," she coos. "Meditate. Love yourself and watch the mind. Bye-bye!" She is so eternally cheerful, dammit!

Hacker is all over me as soon as I click off. "Hey, let's do it, dude! Lemme have a crack at this babe! You hold the door to her room closed and I'll hop into the sack wid 'er! D'you know how to disconnect an I.V.? Maybe she has a roommate and you can get a little too?"

"Hacker, I am a married man," I say indignantly.

"Yeah, right," he replies with a sneer.

Sometimes my friend Hacker is a disgusting, amoral human being.

CHAPTER FOUR

In Search of the Goddess

Los Angeles
1986

I returned to L.A. a couple of weeks after the Tantra group. The Indian Monsoon had kicked in, right on schedule. It rained for nine straight days, and I couldn't wait to escape.

When I left Los Angeles for India just a few short months before, I left a good job as an editor for *Hustler* magazine. It got pretty weird toward the end. Larry Flynt, the genius publisher, had become a born-again Christian after hanging out with Jimmy Carter's sister. That was weird. Then he wasn't born again anymore, and that was even weirder. My cocaine and beer habit had become highly developed during my tenure at the magazine. I was having a great time, but I couldn't stand myself.

Now, after a few months of intense group therapy, meditation, and exposure to some very cool people in India,

I couldn't go back to that lifestyle anymore. Plus I realized I had a real jones for Ms. Leela. It wasn't just the cosmic sex or those amazing green eyes, it was something else. Love? Naw, I was too jaded just to "fall in love."

I wanted to look for her, but had no idea where to start. For openers, I didn't know her full name or where she lived. In actual fact, I knew nothing about her. All I knew was, there was some kind of connection between us.

Luckily, I was able to get back in my bungalow in the San Fernando Valley, a perfect little bachelor pad. I had to work to pay the bills, and when you have *Hustler* on your resume it's hard to get a "straight" job. So I became a temp—a typist-for-hire, a Kelly Boy, as it were. I could type over 100 words a minute, and wear a white shirt and tie to work without gagging. It was a living.

Meanwhile, I started haunting every meditation center, every headquarters of every spiritual movement, every personal growth enterprise in L.A., in hopes of finding my goddess.

I started at Alcoholics Anonymous, and since I had already dropped drugs and alcohol in India, I re-learned how to drink gallons of coffee and smoke cigarettes at AA. Also met some foxy women and hung out with three ex-writers from Hustler. Did the first three steps and dropped out.

I did a weekend at what was left of est, GOT IT!, and moved onto its stepchild, The Forum. I got hooked up to an E-meter at Scientology headquarters in Hollywood and looked at my engrams, did a Silva Mind Control course, and hung out with the premmies at the Malibu ashram of rotund child guru MaharaJi.

All of this seemed pretty lame after my experiences at the ashram in India, and I still hadn't found my goddess, so I upped the ante a bit: Doing Transcendental Meditation and getting (buying) my personal mantra; chanting and dancing with the Hare Krishnas on the beach in Venice; doing Kundalini Yoga with the White Sikhs; and even chanting "Nam Yoho Renge Kyo" at the top of my lungs with 200 people, which is supposed to bring anything you desire. It didn't work. I tried Zen Meditation and could only sob silently in the total silence of the room.

Nothing worked. My heart ached for my goddess. Instead of meditating, I could only visualize that tall, gorgeous lady with whom I had shared some very intimate moments of bliss.

Every place I went that had some spiritual connection, I asked if they had ever heard of a woman named Leela. Several people had. I tracked down several Leelas, and was disappointed each time. Turns out that Leela is a fairly common name for female spiritual seekers.

Shit! I cried out one night in my lonely bachelor pad, and, feeling like a total loser, decided to start drinking and using again. I also started hanging out with a fast crowd of temps who liked to party every night.

My best temp friend was a guy named Al who cooked and sold crystal meth to supplement his income. He would get absolutely wrecked on beer and speed on most nights, and then report to his various temp jobs in the morning, red-eyed, hung over, and ready to work.

One night he was driving his beat-up old Buick with me and several temps in the car. We were all working for an insurance company in Santa Monica. And we were all toasted to the gills this night. Al ran a red light and we got smacked by a pickup truck. Al sat slumped over the steering wheel; the three women in the car were all screaming, and another temp guy had fallen into the street when his door flew open.

In my sodden and shocked state, all I could think of was to run away, and fast. In the distance a siren wailed. I had a couple of joints in my pocket and one bust for possession on my record already. I ran as fast as I could, toward the side streets, away from the lights and the cops and the temps.

The neighborhood was shabby, a refuge for the homeless and the lost, with tacky storefronts and an adult movie theater on the main drag. Several blocks from the accident, on a dark and quiet street, I saw a building with lights on inside. I moved toward it like a moth to a flame.

People were just leaving, young pretty people, chatting excitedly. I propped myself up against a light pole, drunk, stoned and stunned, and watched. Through my haze I made out some fancy lettering on the window, and the words something-something Meditation Center. Had I entered a state of dream delirium?

After nearly everyone had left, I stumbled inside and promptly fell on the carpeted floor. A young man came over and helped me up, stood me upright, and looked me up and down. I was bleeding from the head and my shirt was torn.

"Whoa, big guy," he said, holding me up. "Wha happened to you?"

"Uh, ish a— ish a long long long long story," I managed.

"I'll go get a washcloth and let's clean you up a bit," he said. His accent sounded Dutch, or something else European.

As he dabbed the cold cloth around my sad, wounded head, he stopped suddenly and grabbed my shoulders and looked into my eyes. "Hey, man, were you in India recently?"

"Uh, yeah, I thunk I wash. I mean, I think I'm drink— yeah, I wash. Shure. Why?" I was getting defensive, like drunks do.

"Because I remember you from the Encounter Group! Marty, right? The one who got into that fight with the German, right?"

I nodded. I remembered. This was the guy who had literally rescued me during the group, which in those days permitted mild violence. The big German hated Americans and had knocked me down and tried to sit on my head. We were all naked and it got pretty ugly. My young friend grabbed the German in a headlock and pulled him away before the group leader called the guards. I always felt I owed him a big debt.

"Right," I said. "I'm the one. Thanksh for shaving my ash, by the way," I slurred. We sat down on the floor and faced each other. His eyes were incredibly blue, like crystals, and he seemed to look right into me. He seemed very, very kind.

I had a bright idea. "Hey, man, did you ever do thish Tantra Group in India?"

"No," he said. "No, I wanted to, but my girlfriend at the time wouldn't let me."

"Oh. Hey, man, do you know shomeone named Leela?"

"Leela? Sure! She just got back from Mexico. Left her husband, finally, went to Mexico with some girlfriend, now she's back."

My heart started pounding so fast I thought the good Lord would take me home right then and there. "And—

and— ish she kinda tall and gorgush and got green eysh and—"

"That's her, yeah. Do you know her?"

"Uh, yeah, I did, kinda. Back in India. Where ish she now? When can I shee her, good buddy?"

"She's probably home, Marty. She was here earlier for the celebration. She's got a new boyfriend and is probably hanging out with him. Plus, I don't think you want to see her in the shape you're in."

"A new boyfriend, shit shit shit," I muttered. I started to cry.

"It doesn't look too serious with the boyfriend," he said. "C'mon, let me take you back to my house. By the way, it's called the Tantra House and a bunch of us live there. Let's get you back in shape and clean you up so you can maybe see Leela pretty soon. Okay?"

"Okay," I muttered. I didn't have too many options at the time. This one sounded pretty damned good.

CHAPTER FIVE

She's Ba-a-a-ck!

Sedona
Present Day

My office is located on one of those quiet residential streets not far from Sedona's main drag, which is called 89A—a strange name for a street, and I suppose the "A" stands for "alternate." One of Sedona's ongoing problems, and only getting worse as time goes on, is heavy traffic on 89A. For a small town, it is a deadly thoroughfare; many have died driving it and many have perished trying to walk across it.

It is our only major road from east to west, the speed limit is an insane 40 mph, and road rage is rampant. A toxic mix of drivers—confused tourists, angry locals, elderly people who shouldn't be driving, and various escapees from south of the border—adds up to a dangerous situation. After dark, drunk drivers weave across the multiple lanes of 89A, sometimes striking other cars and often winding up in police reports.

My office serves mainly to conduct the business of my website. The office is in a guesthouse behind one of those mobile homes that look like real houses. I used to run the site out of our home, but the business got too big and too dangerous. I had to get my own servers to handle the increased bandwidth as we got more and more visitors and more pageviews.

The dead rattlesnake in the mailbox was a reminder of my (our) vulnerability. Sedona is a small town and it's easy for any weirdo to find out where you live.

Nevertheless, business is booming. My Google ads are paying off big-time. Local advertisers, those who don't care that our content is a little controversial, are coming on board.

The site started attracting attention when we began our muckraking articles, then got more notice with our "Rants & Raves" posts from viewers. We captured the Baby Boomer demographic with our "Ask Jessica" column, which provides advice on dating etiquette and other personal issues.

But what really put us over was our online dating service, "Soulmates 4 U." This department has two sections. The first is for those people, mainly women, who are actually looking to find the love of their lives through our service.

It works like all of those so-called social networking sites out there on the web, such as match.com. You post your photos on the site, list a few details about yourself, describe what you are looking for in a soulmate, and wait for the e-mails to pour in. Because of the Sedona angle, Soulmates 4 U generates traffic from all over the world.

But embedded in the Soulmates home page is a

simple little link that has brought our site so much traffic that we had to buy a new server. "Cybersluts" is strictly for people looking for no-strings hookups, either virtual or in the flesh.

It is here that Hacker's genius has made us a leader in the online dating world. He has written a program for Cybersluts that combines the best of YouTube and Second Life.

First, there is video. Members post homemade videos of themselves with only one restriction: nothing illegal or hardcore.

Second, there is the interactive feature. Members are transported to a virtual world called Planet Sedona. There your avatar, bearing the face from your photo and the physical features you describe in our questionnaire, can meet the girl or guy of your dreams, and—yes—*go all the way* with the other's avatar.

By using the telephone or a microphone with your computer, you can have actual, real time conversations with the avatar of your choice. And, by paying an extra fee of only $10 a month, you can download Hacker's Artificial Intelligence software and infuse your avatar with a unique personality. Then you can sit back and watch your digital double have real time liaisons, seemingly acting on his or her own, with the avatars of your choice!

Androgyny, cross-dressing, disguises and gender-switching are surprisingly popular in Planet Sedona's virtual world. Oh, that Hacker! If I ever hit it big with this website and sell it to Google or something, my friend Hack gets a big piece of the action.

On a hot Monday morning, the mad genius bursts into the office with a big grin on his face. Jill, my secretary, looks up briefly and then goes back to her work on QuickBooks. Hacker has been after her since she first went to work for me, but she merely shrugs off his attentions. My friend is a little too, um, rough-hewn for her tastes, and besides he is a too-obvious ladies man.

Jill is about 30 and a real doll. Tall and thin and in great shape, she works out and also teaches yoga. She came to Sedona about five years ago from Nashville after dumping an abusive husband. Like many who come here, she wanted to start a new life in an exciting place where the possibilities seem endless and dreamers are welcome—as long as you can pay the high rents.

Hacker slips into my office and closes the door. He rubs his hands together and giggles with glee.

"So," I ask, my eyes on the computer screen as I try to finish my story about illegal aliens. I hate to be interrupted when I am in creative mode. I do most of the writing myself for the website, but I also have a reporting staff of Citizen Journalists (CJs)—amateur roving reporters who cover the town like a blanket and send in stories that our local media either can't or won't cover. Many CJs also send in videos, which are very popular.

I know that the horndog Hacker has been taking first crack at the women in the Sedona area who have joined up on our Cybersluts link. To me this is like insider trading, but what the hell. Hacker wrote the program, he should get the spoils.

"So," says the Hacker. "That chick from Cornville who is a concierge at one of the timeshares and likes to be ravished by manly men? The one who is into UFOs and angels and spirit guides? Remember her, the sexy pictures on Cybersluts?"

"Yeah. So what?"

"Man, she has fantastic feet! Red toenails! And she loves to get foot massages, says it activates her chakras. And—"

I yawn. "Yeah. I know. Look, Hack, I'm kinda busy right now. Would you check the servers, please? The system is running kinda slow and you may need to add some memory. Also, check the firewall. I sense that someone is going to try another attack, real soon, if they haven't already."

There is something I need to share about John Hack, Jr. He talks about women's feet like most guys talk about boobs or butts or legs or whatevers. He is, and I'll be frank, a foot fetishist. It is said that the first thing men look at in a woman is her face, mainly her eyes. Then the male eyes drift downward.

Hacker starts at the feet! Pretty feet trump everything else! The color of women's painted toenails is a secret code, known only to a few elite foot fetishists. Bright red means naughty, looking for action. Dark red means you better be ready any time I want it. Pink means a tease. Black means—no, I don't want to go there. Okay, it means she is into the dark arts—probably a Scorpio.

The phone rings and Jill buzzes me on the intercom. "It's Leela, Marty. I think she's back."

"Thanks. Hacker? My wife's on the phone. Would you mind...? Uh, don't you have some megabytes to mess with today?"

"I know when I'm not wanted," he mutters, and slams out of my office.

"Hi, sweetheart. Are you home?"

"I am home and I really miss you. Can you come home now? I need to see you. It's important..."

"What's up, dear?" I proceed carefully. She wants to see me now. This is either really great or really bad. Maybe she wants to bust me about the thing with Aura. Or maybe she just wants to make mad passionate love because she's been away for a week.

Leela loves daytime sex. Maybe she wants me on her and in her and all over her, kissing that beautiful satiny skin, her mouth on my throbbing manhood, my mouth bringing her to orgasm after screaming orgasm…or maybe the marriage is over and I'm a dead duck.

Either way, it would be a great adventure. I love the unexpected. "I'll be right home," I say, nearly breathless. "Be ready for me."

I can hear her deep breathing over the phone. "I'm ready now. Hurry."

CHAPTER SIX

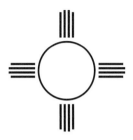

Coincidence

Los Angeles
1987

When Leela was nine years old, she realized that she could see auras. She thought it was just rainbows around people. She told her mother and the mother took her to a so-called specialist, thinking her little girl was autistic.

When she was 12, she discovered that she knew things that others didn't know. She could, for example, deduce the real intentions of the adults around her. She sensed when people were lying. She felt Uncle Harry's evil intent beyond the gifts and smiles and extravagant attentions.

When she was still a teenager she learned how to astral project—how to have out-of-body experiences whenever she wanted—and how to tune in to people's thoughts and emotions. She became an empath without really understanding what was going on.

I learned all of this while sitting on Leela's white-washed deck overlooking the palm trees and shabby apartment buildings in rent-controlled Santa Monica, California. She had scored a somewhat shabby apartment building of her own—six singles, no frills—when she finally divorced her evasive husband.

"I married this guy when I was just 19—"

"A child, really."

"—yeah, a child, 'cause that was just what you did then. They wanted to marry you off, get you out of the house, start raising a family." She made a face; she had never reproduced, didn't believe in it.

"My father had died the year before, so maybe I was looking for a new daddy, too. He was only 53. Hit by a lady drunk driver at 11 in the morning about three blocks from where we lived." She shook her head and looked away.

"My father died at 53 too. Heart attack."

Leela looked at me strangely. "You didn't like your father much, did you. Or rather he didn't like you. He had a terrible temper, right? I'm getting this image of a lot of snow and a little boy almost naked running through the snow being chased by a red monster. Wow."

My jaw dropped open. "Leela, are you psychic or something?" I asked. This was very confidential information, known only to my two former shrinks. That image, the stuff of nightmares, was stored in my unconscious mind. "What else?" I said.

"Well, it was almost an arranged marriage. I'm talking about me, now," she giggled. "Barry was good-looking and came from a good family and had a job in real estate. He was my first man. I was a virgin on our wedding night."

"Jesus!"

"Well, not exactly." Leela laughed, a hearty, surprising laugh from deep in her throat. "And luckily there was no conception, because I was on the pill."

We bantered so easily, as if we had known each other for years. This was our first "date," actually. After my new friend from the meditation center rescued me on that drunken, dangerous night—no one had died in that car accident, fortunately—and taken me home with him to the Tantra House, it took awhile before I was cleaned up and sobered up enough to face the light of day, much less meet my goddess.

It took a month. It was like being born again, leaving behind a broken body and a broken past and given a chance to start afresh. I had blown the temp gigs and got evicted from the Valley pad. My ragged old Toyota had been towed after sitting on the street for a month. I had no money, no job, no home, no car, and no future. I was just a nobody.

It was wonderful.

The Tantra House was a real communal house where six people lived together and shared all of the expenses, cooked for each other and got along beautifully, holding "clearings" whenever there was a conflict. Three women and three men, all holding jobs out in the world, none involved with each other, all meditators.

One of them was Christa, a striking 40-something blonde from Sweden, who took a shine to me and helped me through my recovery. She was a massage therapist who worked at a big resort by day, and by night her gentle hands soothed my body and soul.

She often spent the night with me in the little alcove

39

the good Tantra House people had put me in, basically a large closet with a wall-to-wall mattress. Our sex was hot, sweaty, and intense, with a chorus of loud shrieks and moans from her when she climaxed, which was several times each session.

One morning, in the bathroom I shared with Christa, I looked hard into the mirror and saw someone I barely recognized.

So...here you are, man, clean, sober, not even thirty, piercing blue-gray eyes, lots of nice curly hair, a lean and mean six-footer, feeling great for the first time in months...are you gonna fuck up this scene? No!

I'm off the sauce, off the blow, looking for my goddess, go go go! Why do I fuck up? Must be my DNA. Russian-Polish genes, no wonder I lean toward the dark side. My father, poor bastard, with his failed, small-town dreams. But I'm lucky, I coulda been stuck with the name Moishe Polski.

Talk about getting lucky, this gentle Christa with the hard body, these beautiful people, my goddess somewhere out there, close by. What did that Indian guru say? Love yourself and watch. Watch what? The mind, the mind, the friggin mind. The terrible monkey mind. Be the watcher. And don't forget to breathe.

Near the end of my month-long recovery period, I came to Christa, guilty and embarrassed, and asked if she minded if I saw Leela. She laughed. "I will call her for you. Are you sure you are ready for her? Maybe you should come to the meditation center tonight. We are having a Full Moon celebration. She will probably be there."

She was. I was sitting quietly in a corner, waiting for the evening meditation to begin, when Leela walked in. Actually, it was more like a royal entrance. She wore a long, dark red robe fringed with faux fur at the collar and at the bottom. Her raven hair now hung halfway down her back. She carried herself like a queen at a coronation, elegant and regal and in her power.

She saw me, flashed me a look that I took to be either recognition or dismissal, and moved into the room with some loser on her arm. This guy, shabby, bearded and wimpy, wore the male counterpart to Leela's robe. On him it looked like a joke. He walked with a noticeable limp. The evening passed; I kept to myself, and didn't have the nerve to approach her.

Later, Christa told me that Leela's "boyfriend" was just a stray that Leela had taken in, a former lover who had fallen on hard times. He would be gone soon. Leela seemed to have lousy taste in men, but at least she had compassion.

Three days later I lounged in the afternoon sun on Leela's balcony on our first date and grew ever more intrigued. She wore white shorts, exposing those long and shapely legs, and a tank top which revealed a breathtaking cleavage. I had experienced her nakedness in India, but this was different.

"Where are you from?" she asked absently.

"Omaha. You know, Nebraska. Hicksville. And you?"

"Omaha too. Ha ha! I was only born there, didn't live there long."

My heart started pounding. "What hospital were you born in?" I asked, almost afraid to hear the answer.

"Uh, I think it was the Methodist Hospital. Yep. Methodist. And you." She said "and you" as a statement, as if she already knew the answer.

I gulped. "Uh, yeah. The. Methodist. Hospital. On Leavenworth Street, I think."

She closed her eyes for a full minute. "And—don't tell me—the doctor who delivered you was…Dr. Taylor," she said. "Right?"

"How did you know that?" I nearly shouted. "Are you really psychic? Wait a minute. Your doctor was—oh, no, this can't be, this is way too much of a coincidence—Dr. Taylor?" She nodded.

We both leaped up, had a huge hug, and started jumping up and down, laughing and screaming. I was afraid we would go right through the rotted wooden deck.

"Does this mean we are—" I stopped, almost in midair— "that we are, uh, like, soulmates?"

"Sure," she gushed, "I guess so. Yeah, we're soulmates. At least for now. Soulmates. I like that. Hmmmm…" she said with wrinkled brow.

We had a wonderful afternoon, but she sent me packing at sunset because she had another date. Long story short, two weeks later I had moved in with Leela. We squeezed into one single apartment since she rented out the other five to pay the mortgage.

She worked in the movies and in TV as an extra and also continued to see two other boyfriends. Sometimes she would be gone for four or five days at a time, but she always called to "check in" at least once a day.

I signed up with some temp agencies on L.A's west side, bought a used BSA 650 motorcycle to get around, and settled in for a wild and wacky new way of life. I was in love—so I thought. But life with Leela was totally unpredictable, and totally amazing. I knew I was in for one wild ride.

42

CHAPTER SEVEN

My Wife the Precog

Sedona
Present Day

HOW TO SOLVE THE ILLEGAL IMMIGRANT PROBLEM IN SEDONA

Round 'Em Up, Send 'Em Back to a Prosperous Mexico

Why can't our neighbor to the south become the new China? All of the necessary elements are in place: a large and willing labor force, access to raw materials, huge amounts of investment capital, and a built-in market to the north: the good ol' USA.

The problem with Mexico is the same situation we have been dealing with for generations: extreme poverty and a hopelessly corrupt government. Today Mexico is basically a failed state, a narco-state that exports its woes

43

across our borders. This includes not only megatons of marijuana and bad drugs such as meth, heroin and cocaine, but also desperate people who will risk their lives to reach the promised land.

If they make it across our leaky border, they fan out across the U.S. Many make it to Sedona. There is a lot of work here for immigrants, legal or illegal. Most of their income is sent back to their home country of Mexico. Their government both encourages and appreciates this arrangement.

Because of articles like this one that I regularly post on my website, my wife thinks I am a bigot. She also feels that overall, I am too negative. She also fears that by tackling such controversial subjects I will get us both into big trouble.

She might be right. The dead rattlesnake in the mailbox was an ominous warning. I attribute that to an article I posted claiming that several Sedona businesses—including contractors, resorts and restaurants—were not only hiring illegals, but also stuffing them into rented "safe" houses, abusing them, and sometimes not paying them. As a direct result of this article, arrests were made, people were deported. A rattlesnake was sacrificed.

I run these articles because of a sense of outrage, and because the public, clueless as they may be, have a right to know. My wife, like most women, prefers a more passive approach to conflict. We males are ready to shoot each other, or to club each other senseless over food, turf and women, as we used to do at the dawn of civilization.

So my website, and the provocative articles I choose to run, cause some major disagreements in our house. Of course we have other issues. For one, Leela's career as a

44

psychic. While I acknowledge that she is very intuitive and no doubt has some psychic powers, I continue to scoff at the woo-woo aspect of it all.

Sedona *is* woo-woo world headquarters. To me, the psychic readings business in our town is some sort of a scam. That is my personal opinion. And Leela is deeply involved in it.

Still, in spite of these differences, she loves me. And I love her. Our love is forever, we both declare. We actually take this soulmate stuff seriously. I criticize her for being terminally cheerful, and because she refuses to see the reality of the human condition. I also remind her that she is a little too generous in handing out B.O.D.—Benefit of the Doubt—to too many people who don't deserve it.

"Did you see that asshole cut me off? He's doing 60 on 89A and not bothering to signal!" "Well, he's probably late to work or in a hurry to get home to his wife and kids." This is B.O.D.

Occasionally I have to remind her, as well as myself, that opposites attract. That is basic physics. And there is no doubt that we are fiercely attracted to each other.

Her homecoming from Flagstaff was a joyous, memorable occasion. We spent the entire afternoon bouncing around on our new king-size bed, rewriting the Kama Sutra. It was 105 degrees outside, but super cool in our air-conditioned love nest.

We finished the afternoon in that legendary Tantra position, face to face, loins locked and loaded, soaring off into that bliss state beyond time and space. And a wonderful reminder of the first time we "did it" in India.

Best of all, there was no mention of my little indiscretion—better make that plural—with her friend Aura. So

I figure it's one of two possibilities: That she is granting me *enormous* B.O.D. Because she knows about it because Aura blabbed. Or because Leela can see right through me. Or she just flat doesn't know or suspect because I am such a loving husband and an honorable citizen.

Leela may have psychic powers plus tremendous insight and intuition, but she doesn't know everything. And I seriously doubt that she can really read minds. I'm not carrying around a load of guilt on my shoulders; my eyes are not cast downwards, I have no noticeable tics, and I do not go to confession. Leela and I both agree that sex is an energy phenomenon and not a moral issue.

"Just don't fuck my friends," she once blurted out. Oops!

I am called to Judgment Day. There is a long line at the gate. I have always hated long lines, but there is no complaining here. I finally get to the front of the line. Instead of St. Peter it is Jack Nicholson, wearing his vestments, looking paunchy and wasted.

"Come forward, boy," he thunders, in that killer voice from The Departed. *He looks me up and down. "So," he says, reading from a piece of parchment, "it says here that you fucked your wife's best friend. Is that correct?"*

"Uh, no sir, Mr. Peter, uh, I mean Jack, sir. Okay, you got me there. Yes, I f-f-fucked my wife's best friend."

"Hmmmmm," says the overweight angel. "Did you at least use a condom when you banged this broad, boy?" he says, those hyperactive eyebrows twitching and jerking.

"Uh, uh," I stammer, trying to buy time. But there is no time to buy. Not on Judgment Day. "No, no sir, I didn't have a condom with me. Plus she was on the pill."

"Fuck you, boy!" the angel yells in my face. "You can go to hell!!"

Leela's psychic career is really taking off now. She works two or three days a week at the Crystal Palace in Uptown, charming and astounding the tourists with her skills and insights. She uses a couple of Tarot decks, numerology, astrology, and the pendulum to give her clients, usually women, advice on love, money, and careers—the top three questions for most psychic readers. This is more like entertainment.

She also does the more serious stuff associated with psychic readers. If a client wants to know how her poor husband Hymie is doing on the other side—if he's happy in his new home in Paradise, or suffering in Hades—she can contact Hymie and get an answer. If you want to know who you were in your past lives, she will put you in a light hypnotic trance and talk to your Alexander the Great or Cleopatra or Wendy the Witch burning at the stake.

She will align your charkas and balance your energy with crystals. She will read your aura and give you a 20-page computer printout on what those funny colors mean. She will contact your angels and spirit guides and give them your cell phone number.

She will answer some of your most urgent questions, such as: Should I leave my husband? Should I leave my job at Wal-Mart and go on welfare? Should I hang myself in the garage? with the use of a pendulum, which gives "yes" or "no" or "I don't know" answers.

But I exaggerate on the garage suicide business. I tell her that some of her clients do need to seek out professional help, go on a non-fat diet of happy pills, or have a prefrontal lobotomy. She agrees, and encourages the most emotionally challenged of her customers to see a shrink.

Leela not only has innate psychic skills, she also

studied for years to learn the tools. She took a year-long esoteric sciences course in Sedona; she got a degree in metaphysics from an online university; she has hung out with shamen and mystics and holy men and women from India to Indonesia to Central America.

She has undergone secret initiations by Sufi masters in Turkish mystery schools, studied Reiki in the U.K. with Druid descendants, and learned the secrets of alchemy from teachers in unnamed places. If she wanted to, she could probably walk on water, bring on the Monsoon, heal the sick and raise the dead.

That is how much I think of this woman, how high the esteem in which I hold her. And yet, I scoff.

We are sitting on the front deck of our cozy house in West Sedona, one of those super-trailers which they call "manufactured homes" here. They look just like real houses, some of them, but they arrive on wheels, in two sections, and the walls are made out of pasteboard and the crawl spaces underneath can be attractive to certain rodents, black widow spiders and occasional families of skunks.

It is late Sunday afternoon. We are enjoying the relative quiet and the view of cottonwood trees, cactus, quail dashing hither and yon with their young, Cathedral Rock and the craggy heights of the Mogollon Rim in the distance. The summer rains have finally come, and nearly every afternoon the clouds turn dark, thunder rumbles in the distance, and lightning flashes dance in the sky.

Today the chance of rain is 40 percent. Some of us have put money on the table. The odds have been set at 3-2 against rain coming by the 6 o'clock deadline. A six-pack of Oak Creek Amber Ale, representing our local microbrewery, and two bottles of merlot decorate the table.

Gathered on the porch are my staff, such as it is: Jill, Hacker, and two citizen journalists, Cole Warner and Benny Bravo, the latter being Sedona's only known Mexican Jew.

Also soaking up the good vibes are three psychic friends of my wife's, and an off-duty Sedona cop friend we simply call Bud. The mood is jovial, and the booze flows freely. I know Hacker is holding some really good weed, and can't wait to break out a big spliff, but I ask him to wait, out of respect for Officer Bud.

"What's your latest exposé, boss?" asks Hacker absently, not looking me in the eye. His eyes are riveted on the many naked female feet in evidence. Painted toenails everywhere. Sahara Starseed, the real hottie of the bunch, is wearing open-toed sandals by Gucci that are driving my friend crazy.

"Uh, I don't want to put my foot in my mouth," I answer, "but—" It's a joke that nobody gets except Leela, who is jabbing her elbow into my ribs. "Well, I thought I'd take on the psychic world next. You know, expose those frauds who exploit our poor tourists. Psychics who cast spells and fake Gypsies who charge people big bucks to take off and put on spells."

The girls are all looking at me funny. "Don't expose me!" says Shakti Pat, an Uptown reader with a large clientele and stunning tits. She is wearing a skimpy halter top and short white shorts, plus bright red toenail polish. Kat Kitman is a pet psychic who can tell you why your dog keeps peeing on your new carpet or why your cat hates your boyfriend. She talks to the animal and gives you a report, only $100 a session.

"No, no, I wouldn't expose you ladies. Ha ha. Ahem." I think the wine is working and I engage my internal editing program so I don't say embarrassing stuff. "Actually, this new series will help you, because the frauds will have to pack up and leave town. More business for you."

"I'm on a piece about corrupt government officials. These people have money invested in the projects they're voting on," announces Cole Warner, a straight-arrow type with a big mustache who used to drive for Pink Jeeps. "It's kinda unbelievable," he adds.

"Hope you got some documentation," says Jill, who is also our fact-checker. "The boss doesn't need a libel suit."

"Right," I agree. "Benny, what you got, homey?" I call him homey due to the fact that he likes to dress like a gangbanger: black tank top, low-slung jeans, tattoos from shoulder to wrist. He plays heavy rap on his souped-up, sub-woofered to the max pickup truck speakers, which has gotten him busted twice while driving down 89A. Bud did an intervention for him both times.

"Yo, homes, I be workin on why the fuzz still bustin locals for smokin weed." He turns toward Officer Bud, winks, offers him a high-five.

Bud gets serious. "Yo, if you fools would just do it in your cribs instead of puffin away on 89A—hey, that rhymes, I should be a rap singer—with broken taillights and expired tags, we wouldn't have to bust your ass. Fool."

"OK, dawgs, I just kiddin," says Benny Bravo. "My story is on the illegals around town and how your local big-wigs got coyotes from over the border on their payroll and how the whole setup sucks big-time. I got people in the community feedin me data. I got pictures 'n' everything. This be a big one, yo."

I am looking at Leela. She is staring into space, oblivious to the world around her. I have seen this look

50

before. She isn't drunk because she doesn't drink. This look scares me.

"Hey, baby, you channeling again?" I say, hoping to bring her back to where the rest of us are at. Everyone laughs, including Leela.

"No...but I have seen something," she says in a strange, faraway voice. When Leela "sees something," everyone and everything stops. Suddenly, thunder crashes loudly, very close, almost on cue. It's nearly 6 o'clock, and the rain feels like it's about to explode from the clouds. The pressure, the humidity, are almost unbearable. Will the rain come on time? The bets are down. Leela speaks:

"I...hear sirens...screaming...see children on bikes. See. Car. Ambulance. Kids in...street. Adults, running around. It's close, close, close....Oh, it's awful...." She slumps back in her chair, hand covering her eyes.

We all fall silent. Leela has this remarkable ability to see events before they happen. Sometimes it's seconds before something happens. More often it's minutes. And lately, she has been seeing days and even months into the future. Call it precognition. ESP. Whatever. It is to be taken seriously.

From what seems like miles away, we hear the squealing of car brakes, a crash, a thud. We are all frozen.

Officer Bud is off-duty, but his cell phone is ringing. "It's just down on Andante," he says. "The 911 call just came in. Two kids on bikes run down by a speeder. Looks bad. I gotta go."

Suddenly a huge lightning flash lights up the afternoon sky. Thunder follows. The rain starts slowly, and soon becomes a deluge. It is five minutes to six. I look out over our yard, composed mainly of cactus and rosemary, juniper and other high desert plants. The yard is now filling with rivulets of water. Hacker scoops all the money off the table. He was the only one who put money on the rain.

Leela now sits silently with eyes closed, as if in a trance. She doesn't gamble, she just predicts. I turn over the business card on which she scribbled some words and numbers at 10 o'clock this morning. It says: "Rain 5:55 p.m."

CHAPTER EIGHT

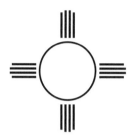

Life with Leela

Los Angeles/India/The World
1988-1996

At first, there were a few old boyfriends coming around for a visit, and Leela's ex-husband, but like a trusty watchdog I soon ran them off. Barry, the ex, was a well-meaning but talkative character. He liked to drop in unannounced for meaningless chit-chats. I had to let him know that I wanted his ex-wife all to myself, now.

Some of Leela's old AA friends also came round. During her marriage she got into drinking too much wine, did The Program, attended meetings for a few years, then dropped out—but never took up drinking again.

I had left much of my past behind me when we moved in together. As her past gradually faded away, we got into our relationship thing hot and heavy. It was a mad love affair from the beginning. Neither of us was much of a drama queen, and we didn't get involved with other lovers, so there wasn't much to fight about.

"Sweetheart," she cooed one morning as we lay in bed after some leisurely sex. "What say we go back to India?"

"Huh? Aw, c'mon, it's soooo far away—and so much trouble to get there." I yawned and rolled over, but she put her sharp, shapely knee into my butt cheeks and rolled me back until I couldn't avoid those penetrating green eyes.

"Listen. I've figured it out. We can take off six months and live on the cheap in India. We've saved up enough money to go. We'll sublet this unit, and the rents will make the mortgage payments. C'mon, you lazy bum."

It was true, I had grown lazy with living the good life. I was still working as a temp, but I had learned the law business and had become a high-priced, full-blown, temp-only-thank-you legal secretary. Leela, meanwhile, had been working as an extra in showbiz and as a model at trade shows; in between she collected unemployment. She also had developed a sideline as a travel agent, which was more like a hobby, but as a result she got big discounts on international flights.

We hadn't been back to India since we had met—make that *connected*—in the Tantra group.

"We can really do it!" She was excited now. "We'll go back to that ashram where we, uh, met, then travel around India on the train. Let's explore. We can visit some holy sites, and go to the Taj Mahal. I've always wanted to visit Varanasi where the people bathe in the Ganges, maybe visit some ancient temples, and we could also go to south India where the Indian Monsoon begins in June."

"How romantic," I humphed. "Listen, babycakes,

India is one big shithole, filthy, crowded, all the food is contaminated, they hate Westerners, we can't even hold hands on the street they're so uptight. You wanna get hepatitis, amoebic dysentery, malaria, cholera, or dengue fever? Take your choice."

I forgot to mention another fiendish disease one could easily pick up in India: giardia. An American guy I met in some group or other at the ashram had acquired this form of rotgut, which is brought on by a nasty protozoa. It is usually caused by—and I quote here—"eating food contaminated by the unwashed hands of an infected person." That would include at least half the waiters and restaurant cooks in any city in India.

One symptom of this disease is unbelievable flatulence. The ferocity of this condition tends to drive away any and all friends and to turn the victim into a social pariah. I liked hanging out with the American, but after giardia got him, he disappeared for weeks into his bleak and roach-ridden room.

Leela pooh-poohed the idea of us getting sick. She is always so goddamned positive! It was early October, a great time to go to India, and so we found ourselves at the Bombay airport in about three weeks.

Finding yourself in Bombay is like being dropped off on another planet, in another star system, far far away. The very smell of the place…egad! A cross between rotting meat and a backed-up toilet. The beggars, the traffic, the foul air, the incredible noise, the sense of a planet on the verge of imploding or just flaming out.

But Bombay (note recent name change back to Mumbai, the old name) is a huge city, India's financial capital, population in the mega-millions. And our favorite ashram is only a few hours away by kamikaze taxicab.

This time Leela and I did not do encounter or Tantra or other such groups. She got herself into the ashram's Mystery School, and learned some skills and esoteric secrets that would serve her well years later. I took hypnosis courses, martial arts trainings, and Sufi dancing.

We meditated, we danced, we partied, and we made love often. India seemed much cleaner, much more welcoming. After three months of fun and good health, we continued our India tour. On the train. Third class. It was Leela's idea. It was horrible. Peasants traveling with real live chickens and screaming babies, eating risky food at train stops, drinking tea and coffee out of unwashed cups. We both got sick and bottomed out in Varanasi. Amoebic dysentery, sure 'nuff, aka "amoebas."

A one-week course on the medication called flagyl got us well enough to catch a flight back to L.A. Flagyl has some very weird side effects: depression, disorientation, loss of self-identity, a generalized feeling that you are somebody else, with amnesia and no past. Back at our cozy love nest in Santa Monica, we quickly recovered our health and picked up the pieces of our life.

We continued our traveling ways for years, Leela and I, six months on the job and six months off for R&R. We returned to India and also did Australia, Bali, Mayan ruins in Belize and Guatemala, Singapore, the Philippines, Japan and on and on.

It helped that she inherited some money from an old friend, and that I managed to squeeze some bucks out of my late mother's estate. It also helped that we saw the bottom begin to fall out of the inflated California real estate market. Actually, Leela saw it coming two years before the crash. We

56

put our home, the creaky six-unit apartment building, on the market and it sold immediately, far above our asking price!

We took our cash and hit the road again. They say travel broadens one, which is certainly true, but if you are *two* you had damned well better like each other. What they call "love" isn't enough. Spending hours, days, weeks in cramped little airplane spaces and hotel rooms and tour buses will test any relationship.

Leela and I never had any problems with this. Neither of us liked to fight, or argue. We both had so many stories from our pasts to share that boredom was never an issue. We could also fall into hours of silence.

I loved her stories about working in movies and TV, because she had worked under some of the top directors in Hollywood, including John Huston, Sidney Pollack, Mel Brooks, Spielberg, Kubrick. She had also been on sets with Elvis, Robert Redford, Ann-Margret, Liz Taylor, Dustin Hoffman. And more.

We went back to our favorite ashram in India, a lovely place with lots of friends and positive energy, and lived there for nearly two years. When we came back to the US of A, we realized we had no place to live—we had sold our home!

Leela and I were tired of traveling and decided to find a brand-new place to live. We still had some money, our health and our good looks. Our mad love affair hadn't cooled off. The idea of marriage had come up, but was not taken seriously.

We looked at a map of the U.S. We were totally burned out on the L.A. scene. We had friends in the San Francisco Bay area, but it was cold there, including the vibe, and super-expensive. Colorado was overwhelmingly right-wing and seemingly owned by the Coors family and the U.S. military. Santa Fe looked good, and we lived there for awhile, but it had serious drawbacks: way too crowded, way too high-speed, and way too hostile.

The hill country of Texas, centered around Austin, was sweet and offered great music and jobs, but it was still Texas. We were lured to the Big Island of Hawaii, and loved it there, but it was too big a jump. We had a few friends in Sedona, Arizona, and assumed it was like the rest of Arizona, as we then perceived it: reactionary, knuckle-dragging gun nuts living a half-life in a desert wasteland fit only for scorpions, rattlesnakes, and giant, mutant cockroaches.

Nevertheless, we drove into Sedona for the first time one terrifyingly hot day in July. This was to become a life-changing energy phenomenon.

Leela and I looked around at the shimmering, electrifying red rocks as we motored north on Highway 179 and simultaneously began shrieking, shouting, laughing hysterically, sobbing uncontrollably, and babbling in tongues.

We had arrived at the Future. For us, Planet Earth shifted on its axis the day we arrived in Red Rock Country.

CHAPTER NINE

Premonitions

Sedona
Present Day

As the long, hot summer grinds on, the Monsoon stingier than usual but the temperature in triple digits nearly every day, Leela seems to be falling into a deeper and deeper funk. She likes to sit in her big easy chair in the living room for hours with eyes half closed, staring vacantly at the wall.

Buddhist monks who practice this technique call it Zazen meditation. Leela calls it her trance state. She says it is the doorway to remote viewing.

Remote viewing: According to the Skeptic's Dictionary, "remote viewing is the alleged psychic ability to perceive places, persons, and actions that are not within the range of the senses." In other words, good, old-fashioned ESP. The former Soviet Union experimented with this practice to spy on American military installations. Then the CIA jumped in and poured millions into their own remote viewing projects so they could spy on the Soviets. Not much came of these experiments.

Remote viewing is often confused with, but differs greatly from, astral projection. The latter is more closely related to an OBE, or out-of-body experience, and is associated with a very fine silver cord that supposedly keeps one's astral body connected to one's physical body.

You could say that remote viewing is more of a business practice, while astral projection is like taking a vacation.

At the recent psychics' conference in Flagstaff, Leela dazzled the crowd with a demo of remote viewing. Basically it was just her parlor tricks—finding which lady belonged to which handbag, what is in a guy's wallet, that sort of thing—but it made the Flagstaff paper and then got picked up by the Associated Press, which meant nearly instant fame.

A blogger headlined his post about her, "The New Lady Criswell?" Leela was not pleased. But one thing invariably leads to another, and so she has been invited to speak and demonstrate her craft at some major paranormal conferences.

Meanwhile, Leela has been getting e-mails and phone calls from people we never heard of: cops and FBI agents from California to Nova Scotia looking for her help in finding criminals, teenage runaways, bodies, missing children. She has made it clear she is not interested in that kind of work.

Today a guy from the State Department in D.C. left a message. The State Department! Probably looking for Leela's help in I.D.'ing terrorists. Maybe even bin Laden; I heard they have a piece of his DNA.

Whoa! Is my girl ready for such shenanigans? She

seems tired, withdrawn, low energy. Lately, sex seems to be the last item on her list of Things I Like to Do.

I approach her carefully, put a cool hand on her warm brow. I massage her third eye.

"Whazzup, sweetheart?" I ask. "Feelin all right? Is it the heat? Workin too hard?" She has been doing readings two days a week at the Crystal Palace, as well as serving her private clientele, doing phone readings and helping out another psychic with e-mail readings. I figure she must be exhausted, although normally she is possessed of incredible energy.

She looks up at me with those amazing green eyes, that look, that look! It says, "Bear with me, please. I am on to something." I scan her slim body. We have been together for more than 20 years, and I still look at her bod with lechery in my heart. She does yoga, Tai Chi, exercises daily, eats well, takes care of herself. No wonder she still looks great.

Except now she looks tired. "Marty, I am on to something. It's big. We may need to take a trip." These words are a euphemism for *I am having another premonition and I need you with me.* In the past, such premonitions had led to:

1. An urgent flight to Glastonbury, England, and a trip to Stonehenge to meet with some Druids who passed on some ancient knowledge.

2. A hike halfway up Sedona's Thunder Mountain to meet a shaman who had just made an amazing discovery of Indian ruins.

3. Leaving a restaurant on 89A seconds before a drunk driver plowed through the window and into the booth where we had been sitting.

I could go on and on. In other words, when Leela speaks, everyone listens. Let me say again that I really believe she has psychic gifts, that she can look deeply into people and see through all their defenses and layers of personality, and that she *probably* has highly-developed ESP skills.

And I don't mean she can see inside people's minds, or read their thought forms, their ideas and fantasies like some of us read the *New York Times*. I don't think so. But she is probably clairvoyant, which means the ability to see things beyond the range of the power of human vision, or in other words, precognition.

Yes, she does predict—but privately, quietly, not as an ego trip or to show off, but it is *just what she does*. Let's just say that she has developed her potential as a highly evolved human being!

"What kind of trip do you want to take, dear?" I ask cautiously.

"You ever hear of that portal supposed to be out on the old Bradshaw Ranch?"

"Portal? You mean like a doorway where you can see into other worlds? That kind of portal?" I am afraid of where this is heading.

"Yeah. That kind of portal."

"When I hear portal I think of the paranormal, UFOs, Skinwalkers, teleporting, alternate universes, cattle mutilations, orbs, strange voices in the night, weird lights, gray aliens, black helicopters. That kind of shit?"

"Yeah. That kind of shit."

"And...you want us to *visit* this portal—*go through it* or something?"

"That's right. In a couple of days. You and me and

maybe Hacker and Jill. A day trip."

"Uh."

"Marty, you know I haven't been sleeping well lately. One reason is I've been visiting the portal—I mean where it's located now. It's not on the Bradshaw Ranch. At least not anymore. It got moved. Maybe too many tourists went there after the guy's book came out. Or maybe it was never there in the first place. Now I'm pretty sure it's right in the middle of some Indian ruins out near Boynton Canyon."

"You've been visiting— You've barely left the house lately."

"Remote viewing, dear. You know, remote viewing."

"Oh. You know, Leela"—my stern voice, here—"you know, you've been getting into some pretty deep woo-woo lately. I am getting a little worried about you. You get into this stuff too deep and they're gonna put you in some whacko farm somewhere and keep you tranked up 24/7." I knew this would piss her off, but I didn't care. I had to say it.

"You know, Marty"—her brittle, kinda scary, really pissed off, rising-in-intensity voice here—"you've been on my case about being a New Ager ever since we moved to Sedona. I've made us a lot of money being a psychic and I've done it without your help. You make fun of me and you laugh at me, and I don't like it! So just fuck off!"

Now, a lot of women I have known would start crying at this point, out of rage and frustration, stomp out of the room, lock themselves in the bedroom and cry it out or storm out of the house, get in the car, peel rubber up the street, and go to a girlfriend's house, where the two of them would rip the male species to shreds for hours; and then come home and go to bed without a word.

Not my Leela, and not this time. She sits solidly in her chair and burns into my soul with those green eyes. *I* leave the room, but I don't cry. I shoot some baskets in the back yard for half an hour and then come back in the house.

Humor is the last refuge of the male scoundrel. We know that women really dig a man who can make them laugh. I walk in with a big grin on my face and start talking as if only a few seconds have elapsed. Leela is reading a paper by Edgar Mitchell, the astronaut who has been talking up the scientific basis of what I sarcastically call woo-woo.

Leela looks up slowly. "At least you're not astral projecting," I offer as a call for truce. She laughs. She puts the paper down and laughs louder, then motions to me to come over and sit next to her on the big easy chair.

I stroke her hair tenderly, kiss her eyes, nose, lips, chin. She holds me tight. "Just support what I'm doing, okay? Just trust that I know something, okay?" She is in her little girl mode now.

"I'm sorry about the woo-woo stuff," I say, and I mean it. "At least you're not channeling like your friend Aura. She gets struck by lightning and thinks she has been invaded by orbs of a higher consciousness from the twenty-third dimension or something! She told me she is channeling a being called I-Am."

I catch my breath and look away. I am sorry as soon as the word "Aura" has left my lips.

"You know, I have been having some strange dreams about Aura lately," she says slowly. "Actually, you and Aura."

I gulp silently. Leela is staring into space.

"You are both swimming underwater with huge waves breaking overhead, and then comes lightning flashes, and thrashing around like sharks have got you, and there's a whole bunch of eels with glowing eyes, and— and— that's all I remember. I had the same dream twice. I have no idea what it means. I haven't been able to get back there. Maybe I should try lucid dreaming."

"Jeez. I don't know what it means, either. Sharks?"

"By the way," says Leela, "how come you and Hacker never called or visited Aura when she landed back in the hospital? She said she felt abandoned by you guys."

I jump up. "I think I hear my cell phone ringing. I better get it. Waiting for a call from Hacker." I head for my office off the living room.

"Tell Hacker we're going to the portal in a couple days, okay?" she shouts after me. "And be sure to ask Jill if she wants to go. Encourage her. I want a balance of female and male energies."

My forehead is beaded with sweat and my heart is pounding as I flop down in my big office chair. Damn. I should never mention that woman's name. Aura, Aura. What happens when I *see* her again? I gotta get beyond this. Hey, how about…meditation? Sitting silently and watching the mind? What a concept!

CHAPTER TEN

Red Rock Fever

Sedona
1996-1999

We rode into Sedona in the middle of July like two grimy cowboys on tired horses looking for a grubstake and a flophouse. Our tiny, cramped Honda Civic—no air conditioning, no radio, one window that would roll down but not back up—had made it through the broiling California desert.

One look at the red rocks and...boom! An epiphany. The locals call it Red Rock Fever.

Driving into town on Highway 179 off the freeway, you first get a taste of red rocks in the so-called Village of Oak Creek, an unincorporated little bastion of unchecked development. This is actually Sedona Lite. The real City of Sedona is still seven miles up ahead, but the views along the way make you a believer.

We had arrived home. We were in love: with each

other, and with this sunny, mysterious little jewel of a place. And we had just arrived!

Having sold Leela's decaying apartment complex, we were now homeless, and Sedona looked like a good place to drop anchor. We knew a few people in town, and the natives seemed friendly. This was back in the mid-nineties, when you could still drive down the main street without risking your life.

We rented a two-bedroom house at the top of Coffee Pot Drive, a little love nest with a view, lots of traffic outside and several varieties of ants sharing the space with us inside. There were plenty of jobs advertised in the local paper, the *Red Rock News*, and the average starting pay seemed to be between $5 and $6 per hour. We quickly discovered a few facts about Sedona:

1. Lots of people know about this place, and millions of them visit each year.

2. Sedona's economy is based on tourism.

3. Everyone pays tourist prices for everything, including locals, who numbered about 7,000 when we arrived.

4. Wages stink, the theory being that it is a privilege to live in this slice of paradise, so bring your own money. Also, Arizona is a right-to-work state, which means, so goes the joke, the right to be poor.

4. Sedona is ruled by developers, contractors, and peddlers of real estate. Also timeshares. Very big.

5. You can no longer buy a copy of *Playboy*, *Penthouse*, or *Hustler* in Sedona. Which says something about the white bread, hyper-moral consciousness that rules this town.

Nevertheless, we decided to stay. Leela got a sales job in Uptown, the tourist ghetto, at $6 an hour plus a tiny commission. I got a job as a weekend DJ at an underground dance club, and a day job as a waiter at the town's only vegetarian restaurant. We managed to scrape by.

After a few weeks, Leela and I came to realize one more fact about Sedona: It might be the New Age capital of the USA, if not the entire world! The town was filled with psychics, mystics, prophets, shamen, lightworkers, clairvoyants, channelers, healers, and spiritual cults of every persuasion. There were at least two mystery schools in town. Famous gurus and spiritual superstars, such as Ram Dass and Deepak Chopra, often came to speak.

Leela and I liked to lampoon the New Age—we had played with the concept in L.A. at a weekly theater improv event we staged, and also on our cable TV show. We thought Sedona would be the perfect place for such pie-in-the-face humor, and so we put on our Zen Cabaret event at the underground dance club.

"There's a psychic on every corner here," said Leela. "Yeah," I said. "I saw one of them the other day holding up a sign that said, 'Will channel for food.'" These and other groaners earned us a sizable audience for awhile, but the numbers soon dwindled and the few tourists who showed up didn't get it at all.

But we loved Sedona and its wacky lifestyles, its possibilities, and best of all, its proximity to nature. Sedona is one of the best hiking places on the entire planet, and Leela and I, big outdoorsy types in our own modest way, joyfully explored the hundreds of trails. We also loved to take naked dips in secret swimming holes in beautiful Oak Creek.

But we grew restive because of our puny cash flow. We decided to buy a house. We had enough left in our savings to make a down payment, but not enough on-the-books income to look good to the mortgage companies. The first two turned us down flat, saying we "didn't fit into the right box."

So I got a second job as a Jeep tour driver and Leela got a second job at a crystal shop as a saleslady and we cooked our books and jerryrigged our financial statement until the money lenders couldn't turn us down. One of them finally agreed to loan us about a hundred grand. In those days, you could still buy a home at a decent price in Sedona.

Leela looked around and saw a lot of psychics raking in a lot of cash in New Age Sedona, and decided she wanted a piece of the action. We both knew, after hanging out together for several years, that she had some unusual psychic skills. So she polished her tricks of the trade—Tarot, astrology, palmistry, dowsing, numerology—and went to work.

The year was 1999, and we were ready to party. First, we decided to get married—for no good reason, except as a lark and, secondarily, to act like grownups and protect our financial fortress. Next, Leela got her first psychic job at the crystal shop where she had labored as an underpaid clerk.

And I, one lonely night when Leela was in L.A. visiting her aging mother, I went alone to The Brewery, which happened to be next to where the old underground dance club was located. This was our local microbrewery, which had grown into a venue for musical acts and had also blossomed into an outdoor beer garden and meeting place for locals.

Their beer kicks your ass, and is to Budweiser and Coors as a BMW 320i is to a Ford Pinto. I was well on my way to 5.0 beer heaven when I noticed a guy at the next table talking loudly to his friends about women's feet. Our eyes met.

"Hey, man, can you dig pretty feet?" he asked me. He seemed about half-gone, but he got my attention.

"Uh, yeah, I guess you mean women's feet?"

He laughed uproariously. "I'm not talking about your feet, big guy! Hey, c'mon over here and join us!"

And so I met the very strange, very alive, very stony character named John Hack. At the time he was a driver for the High Desert Trolley, but he was always on the verge of getting fired on that gig so a couple of years later he became one of the first website designers in town.

Hack and I became fast friends and he turned me on to some of the best hikes in the forest that surrounds Sedona and some Indian ruins that had been otherwise undiscovered and untouched for a thousand years. He used to say that hiking in Sedona was better than any psychedelic drug.

As the 20th Century limped to a close and the New Millennium drew near, it became obvious that big changes were in the wind for America, for Sedona, and especially for Leela and I.

She saw it all coming. She put it in writing. Not surprisingly, she was right. Again.

PART II

CHAPTER ELEVEN

Into the Palatki Portal

Sedona
Present Day

The road called Boynton Pass is a nightmare. It used to be eight miles of bone-jarring washboard, marked by deep ruts and sharp rocks that could knock your fillings loose or destroy a tire. Now it is only about seven miles of the above nightmare, since a new development of homes and golf courses for the super-rich has invaded the forest.

One of the conditions for the developers to desecrate our sacred land was that they pave part of the rutted road. They did. But in the bargain we lost a great hiking trail, and the summit of nearby Doe Mesa will soon feature 360-degree views of mega-million dollar homes and a golf course instead of trees and red rocks.

But what the hell. Progress is progress, and business is business. We are on our way to the Indian ruins at a place called Palatki, which is a Hopi word for "red house." Palatki has some of the best petroglyphs and pictographs in the world that can be viewed by the public. These are ancient etchings in the rocks that look like animals, people, and things. Rock art, it's called. Some of it dates back at least 11,000 years; some experts say it goes back 40,000 years.

The cliff dwellings at Palatki have been restored by modern man and you can still climb around in them. They date back to around 1100 and were built by the Sinagua Indians, probably the precursors to the Hopi.

The mood in the car is surprisingly jovial, considering that we are heading into god-knows-where via a mysterious means that may not even exist. I am navigating our four-wheel drive Jeep Cherokee over the ruts and jagged rocks. "Welcome to the new frontiers of consciousness!" I yell cheerfully and sarcastically. Leela, sitting up front with me, throws me a frown that could fry a neuron.

Hacker and Jill are in the middle seats, chatty and nervous and excited. He wanted to bring his new girlfriend, the one he met through our online dating service, but Leela wouldn't hear of it.

"Too risky," she had declared. "Risky!" Hacker had protested. "What about the risk to me, to Jill?" Leela told him that since they worked for her husband—me—they were covered by liability insurance in case they went mad or broke a kneecap. Hacker had quietly accepted that. As had Jill.

"Tell us again," Hacker says now from the back of the Cherokee, "just why you need to go into this, uh, portal thingy. This porta-potty thingy." He giggles hysterically at his joke, obviously stoned.

"Like I told you," Leela explains patiently, "I'm not even sure it's at Palatki. The Native Americans say there is a doorway in the rocks at the end of a trail there that leads into other dimensions. If it's true, I need to go into it. I need to find out something that is very important. I would like you guys to experience it too."

"What's it supposed to be like?" asks Hacker.

"Is it psychedelic?" I ask.

"Hey, I've done acid and mescaline and peyote and mushrooms and ayahuasca and— you name it, I've done it," says Hacker. "Nothin scares me anymore. How 'bout you, Jill? Ever get high?"

"I used to smoke pot in my younger and wilder days," offers Jill, "but I didn't inhale!" She giggles. "Actually, I used to like to take E—Ecstasy—and go to clubs and shake my booty all night. Now I get high on yoga and drinking wheatgrass juice."

"You'll do well in Sedona," I say. I too had ingested a variety of psychedelic drugs in my time, before falling under the spell of the devil drug cocaine. I had also pushed the envelope of consciousness with offbeat meditations, 48-hour sleepless marathons and some reckless experiments with my precious brain, but I have to admit I am trembling inside as we approach the so-called Palatki Portal.

Leela has blithely ignored our questions about the psychedelic effects of the doorway to other dimensions. I can feel her vibe: she is tremendously excited about having some kind of profound experience in the portal. If it exists.

Finally, we move slowly past the Forest Service kiosk at the Palatki site as I flash my press pass. The portly, yang-looking lady guard waves us in. You need a reservation to get into this place now because so many idiots have etched graffiti over the timeless rock art and desecrated the cliff dwellings.

The four of us wander about, looking like jaded

tourists, wearing our shorts, T-shirts and sandals. Palatki is actually fascinating. You can feel the ghosts of the ancient ones here. The rock art is in one section, nearly a thousand line drawings in all, and the cliff dwellings take you up a gradual incline to a red rock shelf where human beings once lived a marginal existence. The Sinagua (Spanish for "without water") occupied this land for about 300 years until they mysteriously disappeared in the 15th Century.

Leela tells us to look for a particular landmark, a piece of rock art that she saw in a vision that indicates the portal is nearby. It is the ancient sun symbol of a Native American people called the Zia: a sun with rays stretching out from it in four directions. It is also the logo on the state flag of New Mexico.

We wind around and through the cliff dwellings. No one else is around. It is hot and very quiet. Jill sees the four directions logo first.

"There it is! There it is!" she cries. The Zia symbol is about eight feet up a red rock wall, plain as day. It is probably contemporary and has apparently been a little retouched.

Jill seems very anxious to explore the portal, and Leela is like a psychic on a mission. Hacker and I hang back a bit. Where the hell is it?

"A shaman I know told me what the elders believe," says Leela quietly. "He said that this doorway is where the spirits of the mountain made the journey between their world and ours." She closes her eyes and goes silent for what seems like forever. The heat is stifling. "I have a feeling it's right around this corner."

We go around a huge rectangular hunk of rock just beyond the Zia symbol. Dead end. Or is it? In the shadows formed by the rock is a little alcove, totally in darkness. I break out my flashlight and look around. A rock bench, strange markings on the wall, a gloomy, damp, eerie feeling. I back out quickly, bumping my butt against a jutting rock.

"That's the portal?" I ask Leela in amazement. "Do we just go in there and then pass through solid rock into the twenty-third dimension, or what?"

She laughs. "No, silly, we don't pass through anything, except maybe time and space. You just sit down on the rock bench, close your eyes, go inside, and quiet the mind. Just like meditating in the red rocks. Go as quiet as you can, and see what happens. I'll go first. If I'm not out in, say, 15 minutes, come in and get me."

Leela enters the alcove. The rest of us plop down in the hot sun with our backs against a red rock. It must be at least 100 degrees out here. I look at Hacker; he shrugs and shakes his head. I look at Jill; she is grinning from ear to ear, as if she is in line for the best E ticket ride at Disney World. My heart is pounding. I stand up and pace back and forth in the small space.

In less than a minute Leela stumbles out, looking about half-mad, a lopsided grin creasing her face. "Omigod! Omigod!" is all she manages to say. I grab her and hold her tightly next to me. She is trembling and soaked with sweat. "How long was I gone?"

"About a minute. What happened in there?"

"It felt like hours, maybe days, years, eons, hard to say. I'll t-t-tell you later what happened. But I was right! I was right! Great God Almighty, I was freakin right!"

What she was right about I have no idea. I take Jill by the hand and guide her to the alcove. "Wish me luck, boss," she sings. "Leela, what do I do in there? What's gonna happen?"

Leela is still breathing heavily. "Just do as I told you. Close your eyes, get real quiet, and just wait. Maybe—maybe nothing will happen. But when you break through, just remember, you can control it. It's like flying. You"—she has to pause to get a breath—"you are in control of the journey. You go, girl!"

Jill is in the alcove a little longer, maybe two minutes. She lurches out like a drunken sailor. She is laughing and crying hysterically at the same time. She tries to form words but is unable to speak. Her eyes look like she has seen God herself. Leela holds her in a loving embrace as Jill sobs and blubbers.

I look at Hacker and he looks at me. "You go ahead, dude," I say. "I better stay here and make sure the girls are okay. They may need me."

"Du-u-u-u-ude," he drawls, "if I go in there, you go in there, right? I'll go first, and then I'll watch the girls while you go. Right? Right."

When Hacker is like this, you don't argue with him. I nod. He enters the alcove. One minute passes. Two minutes. Three. I look at the ladies. They are blissed out, in their own space, oblivious to everything.

Four minutes pass. "Uh, girls, I don't know how to tell you this, but Hacker has disappeared in the friggin portal! What to do? Leela? Any ideas?"

In that moment Hacker staggers out with a look on his face that I have seen only on the most blissed-out, psychedelicized, seriously stoned acid heads. Or, in more spiritual terms, the looks of those fortunate ones who have received *shaktipat*—energy transmissions—from enlightened masters. He is surprised to see us.

80

"Are— are— you— guys— still here? I've been gone— so long. So long. So far away. So— oh, man, Marty! You gotta get your ass in there now. Now." He falls to his knees, bows to an imaginary deity, his head touching the earth. He sobs uncontrollably. Leela and Jill, their faces soft and wet with tears, look at me expectantly.

"Don't be afraid," says Leela. Because she knows I am. "You'll be fine. Remember what I said. You control the journey."

I look into her eyes in the dim light and see love and reassurance. Jill nods vigorously. I enter the dark alcove and sit cautiously on the rock bench. I close my eyes and suddenly my mind is a runaway train. Thoughts tumble over each other. Dammit! Dammit!! I am afraid to let go! I'm gonna die! I'll never get back! I chant the mantra: Let go let go let go let go let go.…

I go quiet. A sudden flash of golden light. A deafening roar of thunder. Flying. Flying. Here I go!

CHAPTER TWELVE

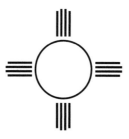

Predictions

Sedona
2000-2004

The New Millennium arrived with a whisper rather than the chaos predicted by the prophets and the paranoids. Leela and I greeted the year 2000 with a long, delicious snuggle in our rented double bed, then decided to have New Year's breakfast at the Red Planet Diner on 89A. It was there that she looked at me strangely and delivered a shocking pronouncement.

"Marty, I have something to tell you. This morning when I was just waking up, I had this kind of vision, like a very real dream, you know? You were still dozing, and I was in this kind of half asleep and half awake space. They say that's the best time to have an out-of-body experience, and other trippy stuff can happen if you keep your awareness. Anyway, it seemed like I was seeing the future."

"So...my little psychic is now becoming a precog,

eh?" I teased. "Tell your daddy what the future holds for us."

Leela smiled indulgently. "There is an election this year, right? The vision I saw was, *The loser wins. The game is fixed.* It was like a big billboard, all lit up and everything. Then it felt like I was going through a time tunnel and I saw all these flashing images of fires and bombs and guns and people dying. I had the strangest feeling that something on the planet had shifted, and we were headed into a very bizarre and dangerous period. All this was connected with the result of the election."

"Wow," I said, suddenly taking her seriously. "'The loser wins, the game is fixed.' That's scary. The election is in November. Al Gore should win easily. But 'The loser wins....' Would you write it down, darling? Put it in your journal or something. We'll take another look at it a year from now."

The year 2000 was a good one for us. We furnished our new house with used furniture and turned it into a cozy home. We worked hard at our jobs and struggled to make ends meet. We hiked, we swam, we met new friends, we had a life.

January 1, 2001—*America falls into a deep sleep this year, until a cataclysmic event occurs around the time of the Autumnal Equinox. I see huge explosions and fires and people screaming and falling out of the sky. This single event changes everything. The leaders use this calamity to gain more and more power, which they use for evil purposes.*

This was the first formal entry in Leela's special journal, the one titled simply "Predictions — for Marty's eyes only." Her confidence boosted by her correct call on the 2000 election, Leela has made her predictions for the year every New Year's Day since. However, most of them are too strong, too real for the public.

She makes her public predictions for the local press, which she has done since becoming a full-fledged, full-time psychic. You know, the usual chestnuts such as relationships, health, prosperity (or lack of it), political upheavals, boll weevils in Bolivia, cockroaches in Casablanca, an air crash over Texas, politicians caught with prostitutes, celebrities headed for rehab, etc.

After the Twin Towers fell on September 11, the world was indeed a different place. As Leela had predicted on January 1, 2001, *This single event changes everything.*

In Sedona, the tourism business simply collapsed for several months as the public stayed hunkered down in their homes. My vegetarian restaurant closed and there wasn't too much work for an old-school DJ; the Jeep tour job was sinking fast. So fortunately I got a job as a driver-tour guide on the High Desert Trolley, maybe the best part-time gig in Sedona. For awhile after 9/11, it was the only tourist attraction doing a decent business.

The trolley holds about 30-some people and is often packed with humanity, so I got a good look at a cross-section of America up close. Too close. I noticed right away that people were truly freaked out after the terrorist attacks, fearful and angry and looking for a fight.

And rude. We Americans have always been a rude, arrogant, aggressive bunch, but the national character seems to intensify when we are under attack by outsiders. The collective psychic energy on the trolley was almost too much to bear sometimes, so Leela gave me charms and potions and crystals for protection, and taught me how to weave an invisible white light around my head.

85

Amazingly, it worked! I was able to block out all the negative energy coming my way, avoid collisions with the legions of bad drivers on the roads, and actually share my love for Sedona with our wide-eyed visitors. The tips were good. Leela's guidance and psychic alchemy kept us in the game.

January 1, 2003—*A rogue king and his lackeys have taken over the kingdom and no longer care what the people think or want. A great war is launched with a seemingly easy victory at first, only to turn into a disaster the likes of which the world has never before seen. Innocents are sacrificed for the war profiteers and the king's rampaging ego.*

And my beloved begins his new career in computing!

My website, SedonaConfidential.com, was launched in October of 2003. The Hacker designed it, and it was a beauty, full of bells and whistles and interactive features and Flash animation, way ahead of its time. Johnny-boy built me a good one, and charged me only a thou. People I knew were paying many times that and getting junk that didn't work, and then the web designers would disappear, taking the access codes and passwords with them. Not the Hacker. He loved Sedona and wasn't about to go anywhere.

I kept my day job on the trolley. The tourists had come back big time. My love-hate relationship with the human race intensified. More and more people needed to consult a psychic, and Leela was there for them. Life was good.

January 1, 2004—*The rogue king clings to his empire while the people cringe in fear. Dressed in cowboy drag, the royal bully swaggers across the world stage with a smoking gun, hurling threats and disturbing the peace. Old rules no longer apply. Government eyes and ears are everywhere. Technology rules. Liars prevail.*

CHAPTER THIRTEEN

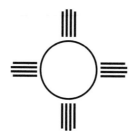

Vortex Energy

Sedona
Present Day

Silence fills our Jeep Cherokee as we head back from Palatki on the bumpy gravel road. We have just experienced something that is, at best, indescribable.

Leela sits up straight, eyes closed, not moving. Behind us, Jill and Hacker sit entwined, arms around each other, heads pressed together. I have to focus my attention hard, engage my brain muscles, to keep from running off the road.

For me, the portal experience started off something like those LSD trips that really took you into an alternate reality, where you could hang out in other dimensions and really *see*: that is, see into and through and beyond the space/time fabric. Where that Oneness you hear so much about, that connectedness between all matter, would be vibrating and palpable.

That was just the opening act and didn't seem to last

long. Of course, in the portal time does not exist and all of the old points of reference are gone and you are left standing naked on a golden platform at the far end of the Universe. Mind is just another software program in the Great Cosmic Computer. I told you the experience is indescribable.

In the rearview mirror I notice that Hacker and Jill are into some serious making out. I tend to think of John Hack as some kind of pervert who women are not turned on to, but just the opposite is the case. He is a real ladies' man.

Tall and lean, with a thatch of graying, curly hair, sporting a fashionable three-day beard, clever and quick-witted, he attracts women like a magnet. And he loves women. I think many of them actually appreciate the loving attention he gives to their feet.

I can't resist, and shout out, "Hey, why don't you two get a room!"

Leela snaps to attention. "Now, sweetheart, I think we're all in a kind of dreamy, stony state and feeling kinda...sensual. Aren't you? I am. Can't you drive any faster? I can't wait to get you home."

"If I drive any faster this poor Jeep will bust an axle and we'll have to spend the night in the woods with the coyotes and rattlesnakes and tarantulas. Would you like that?"

She turns around, pretends to cover her eyes, and says, "You two, just keep on doing what you're doing. Don't listen to Marty. He's just an old poop."

"Leela, darling, what did happen to you in the portal? When you came out you said, and I quote, 'I was right! Great God Almighty, I was right!' What were you so right about?"

"I think I said I was *freakin* right. I was sooooo right

on about my theory. I have to tell you at home, it is very confidential. And it is very very scary. Remind me to tell you what I learned about Google. You know, Google, the search engine, the Web portal. But in the Palatki portal I saw the whole picture about what is going on with the vortexes, and—"

"The what? The so-called energy vortexes of Sedona? The tourist scam that brings the spiritually hungry here by the millions? You mean the four power spots that energize and revitalize and heal the tired and the impotent and the overweight and the lame? You mean those vortexes?" I am on a roll, and just let it pour out of my mouth. I know I'm on dangerous ground here.

"Don't be sarcastic, Marty," Leela warns, with a sharp edge to her voice. "You know I've always believed in the vortexes. A lot of people in Sedona do too. And there *is* an energy here. You've felt it yourself, you said. So don't be so high and mighty and knock the believers."

I need to change the subject, so I turn around to look at our friends. I am a bit shocked by what I see. Their making out has escalated and clothes are starting to come off.

"Marty."

"Yes, Leela." My head snaps back to the front. I have nearly driven off the road.

"I'm sorry I was so sharp with you. I'm still in a weird, sensitive space. Can we go home now? There is a lot I have to share with you. Big, important stuff. Plus, I really want you inside of me."

"Yes, dear." I stomp on the gas pedal, and the tortured Jeep jerks and lurches forward on the washboard road. Soon we'll be on the pavement, and then only 10 minutes, 15 tops, from home. From bed. From secrets revealed.

CHAPTER FOURTEEN

The Magician and the Fool

Sedona
2005

January 1, 2005—*The mighty waters of the brown river, stirred by violent winds, destroy the great city as the rogue king and his minions ignore the cries of the dying. Many more perish from the tidal wave that wipes whole villages off the earth. Wars rage on. The ruler of the Catholic empire goes to heaven. As if to balance the negativity and misery that define the human condition, a new spiritual wave is sweeping across the planet. A lotus emerges from the mud.*

Leela's predictions—those written in her most personal journal—may be for my eyes only, but I know she also has posterity on her mind. Sometimes I tease her about channeling the oblique prophecy styles of Nostradamus and Edgar Cayce, two of her favorite prognosticators.

Truth be told, Leela has been uncannily accurate with her predictions over the years. She says that is because she can "see" what is going to happen on the world stage, usually through dreams or visions or trance-induced states of consciousness.

This doesn't happen when her clients ask her what is going to happen in their lives: will they find their soulmate, succeed in business or find a good job, win the lottery, etc. She likes to use a Tarot deck and let the cards do the work, or she brings out the pendulum to answer difficult questions, or she'll turn to the I Ching if the client is esoterically inclined.

Leela gave me a reading just after New Year's, at my request. I was concerned about my website, and wondered just how far I could and should go in exposing certain people and activities in Sedona. I don't know which deck she used; they all make me nervous. But two cards kept coming up for me, the Magician and the Fool.

Her report, after laying out several hands of the mysterious and mystical deck: The Magician represents the male power of creation. He has great gifts and great power. He can make things happen just by saying "Make it so!" like a certain starship captain. The Fool, on the other hand, represents infinite possibilities, and he is on his way to new beginnings. But he can easily start daydreaming and fall over the cliff, looking like a fool.

Her answer to my question regarding the future of Sedona Confidential: "You can have whatever you want. Declare your intention, stay positive and aware. Don't get into fantasizing or you will stumble. Stay on track."

"But that doesn't really answer my question, sweetheart," I protested. "I need to know if what I am doing with the website will bring danger to our doorstep. If maybe I am pushing this exposé thing a little too far."

"For that question we have to consult the I-Ching,"

she said, with that teasing look in her oh-so-green eyes. "Wait a few days and we'll have a full I-Ching session. In the meantime, do not cross the Great River."

Leela knew that I thought most of the psychic stuff she was involved in was bullshit. But I *was* serious about the readings; I *was* concerned about our future. She went along with it, but I figured she was just playing me. However, she took her psychic work *very* seriously.

Just as I took my website and its purpose very seriously. One thing I enjoyed doing was running stories that our local press wouldn't touch.

SEDONA POLITICIAN'S DAUGHTER BUSTED FOR DRUGS, DUI, SHOPLIFTING

The underage daughter of a prominent Sedona politician has been arrested three times in the past six months for offenses ranging from drug possession to traffic violations to shoplifting.

Because of her age, her name has been withheld by the Sedona Police Department and court records have been sealed until all of the cases are resolved. The young woman has been released to the custody of her parents after the latest arrest, which took place last weekend.

The girl's father declined comment.

This post caused two things to happen almost immediately:

1. A sudden increase in advertising on my site, mainly

nice display ads from local businesses. Some of these business owners told me they were tired of news blackouts in Sedona when prominent or wealthy locals were involved in nefarious activities; and

2. I received the following message on my business e-mail account:

DEAR ASSHOLE

You better be careful what you put out there on the internets. You step on to many big toes in this town and their will be a price to pay.

This I took very seriously, in spite of the spotty grammar and the word "internets" which George W. Bush had invented. This was the first threatening correspondence I had received since the website launched. I called in the Hacker to see if he could track down the source. He said he was busy designing a new online game for a client in Silicon Valley—he called it an ARG, or Alternate Reality Game—but he would take a break and try to help me out.

Twenty-four hours later my good buddy showed up at my house with a six-pack and a big grin on his face. I could smell his homegrown weed on his face and on his clothes. I declined the latter intoxicant, told him I quit smoking because I needed to stay sharp and alert.

He laughed. "Sit down, Marty, I got some news for ya." We sprawled over the couch as he popped a couple of cold ones.

"Whoever flamed you is pretty clever. To put it simply, he or she used a counterfeit e-mail address and a closed account to hide his or her identity. I traced the server source and it supposedly originated in the Virgin Islands. I would just forget it. Take two and hit to right. I guess you like to live dangerously, huh?"

"I am both the Magician and the Fool. My wife told me that. So I know it's true."

"Hey, tell your wife I think she's great. But that purple toenail polish has got to go. Okay?"

CHAPTER FIFTEEN

Whatever Leela Wants, Leela Gets

Sedona
Present Day

It is the hottest sex we have had in a long time, maybe ever, and we have been together for many years. (That portal does make you horny!) Leela is not one of those eyes-roll-up-in-the-head, screaming and howling, blow-the-roof-off type women when she has an orgasm. She is more like, Aha aha aha aha aha...AH! AHHH! AHHHHH! Somewhat polite, but still wild and feral and untamed, just like women should be in their natural state.

But today it's more like riding an endless wave, and I am riding it right along with her. She must have come 20 or 30 times already, but who's counting? I've been rock-hard for about an hour. If this goes on any longer, I may have to call my doctor.

Finally...This could be the big one! It is! Omigod! Me too! I am howling and uttering gutteral, animalistic sounds and Leela is talking in tongues! Together! Together! This. Is. IT! Eeeeeyooooow!

Fifteen minutes later. Holding each other gently, tenderly, looking in each other's eyes, kissing, cooing. Trying not to break the mood, I ask in a hoarse whisper, "Now, what is it you wanted to tell me?"

Leela sighs. "Marty, it's real, real important what I've gotta tell you, and it's complicated, and I don't know if—"

"No time like the present." I cup her breast and pull her closer.

She takes a very deep breath, exhales slowly. "Okay. Oh, wow, where to start…. Okay, do you know why it was so important that I go into the portal? To get information. I needed to get some really important information that I couldn't get on— on this level of reality.

"You know I'm been reading some stuff by that astronaut Edgar Mitchell, the man who landed on the moon and had an epiphany and did some experiments with telepathy and—"

"He had a *what* on the moon?" I rudely interrupt. I am rock-hard again. I am trying to listen, but my cock has a mind of its own. Almost against my will, it approaches its target.

"He talks about the quantum hologram," my wife says, almost desperately. "He says that all this psychic stuff I'm involved in, the ESP, the remote viewing, the clairvoyance, the, you know—that it's all real! It's not just a bunch of woo-woo like you thought! That it all has a scientific basis! That—"

She reaches down between my legs. "Oh my God. Oh my God, Marty."

Suddenly I'm on her and in her and it's all over for Leela. Resistance is futile. At first she resists my machine gun thrusts, then joyously joins in. It is a symphony of lust. We are like two hormone-drenched teenagers who have just discovered the joys of copulation. We generate enough heat to set the bedsheets aflame.

In half an hour we are fulfilled, finished, complete. We lie exhausted on our sweat-soaked sheets, then gratefully fall asleep in each other's arms.

Three hours later. It is eight in the evening. We have satisfied our bodies and our souls and our bellies. We sit nose to nose on the loveseat in our living room. Leela is serious now, and I am listening.

"Get this, Marty. Energy and information are two sides of the same coin, according to Edgar Mitchell. There is a universal archive of information. Mitchell talks a lot about resonance. He says we can connect with a quantum field of resonance holographically and get information from all times and all places.

"That means from the Akashic records, channeled material, the collective unconscious, cultural myths, you know, archetypes, teachings from ancient mystics and modern gurus; all information, from all sources. We can all access this information if we have the right key. That's why I had to go into the portal. To get information. To find the key. And I got it."

"No shit." I feel like a stupid slug as those two words escape from my mouth. The glow has worn off. I am back in my sarcastic, male lout mode again. Duly noted. Leela slowly closes her eyes, giving me a generous dose of B.O.D.

"No shit," she says. "Well, lately I've been feeling

some kind of major disturbance in the—well, call it the quantum field, the energy grid of consciousness—something weird is going on out there, some kind of secret buildup of energy that is going to affect everybody on the planet."

"Leela, there is a lot of weird shit going on right now on this planet, and most of it is right out in the open and nobody can stop it. What's your theory?"

"It's not a theory, it's a fact. Listen carefully. First, the vortex definitely is real. There is now scientific proof that what we call a vortex really *is* a power spot, with an energy source deep beneath the earth. They say Sedona has four of them, but there really are about a dozen power spots in this area.

"And there are thousands of power spots in the world. Each one is like an electrical generator. And, call it coincidence or whatever, the ancient people liked to build their temples, their sacred burial grounds, their places of worship on or near the vortexes of the world. Including here in Sedona. You know, the Native Americans."

I can't handle this. My wife is delusionary. I stand up abruptly. "Leela, for chrissake.…"

"Sit!" she orders, taking my hand and pulling me back into the loveseat.

"Shit," I mutter, like a whipped puppy. I sulk. Finally I manage, "Okay, please continue." Sharp exhalation of breath.

"Listen, baby, the best is yet to come. Stay with me. Pretend it's a sci-fi movie. Okay, so we have nature's energy-generating stations located around the world. Now, what connects these generating stations, these power spots? Ley lines."

"How do you spell that?"

"L-E-Y. Of course the ancients knew all about these ley lines. The Romans and the Indians and the Druids built roads over them. Chaco Canyon in New Mexico is a perfect example of the existence of ley lines. Dozens of roads built in absolutely straight lines for 30 or 40 miles for no apparent reason. They didn't have cars in the 15th Century or whenever. Or even horses, until the Spanish brought them here. But these roads connected their *sacred ceremonial temples.*"

She says these last three words slowly and with such incredible profundity that she could have been saying *Jesus was a Jew.*

"So ley lines are the Earth's natural energy lines. They're like invisible electricity cables hidden in the earth. They are everywhere, a huge grid, all over the planet. You can't see them. But they are there."

"Wait a minute—"

"Hold on, here's the best part. If it's really true that the vortexes are connected by these natural energy lines, what we have is an invisible power grid under the earth of potentially limitless energy—a source of energy that could be used for the common good, or potentially used for destruction. And I mean enough energy to fry this planet to a crisp in seconds."

"Leela, do you remember that great movie 'The Thing from Another World' from the Fifties with James Arness as this giant alien carrot from another planet and the only way they can kill it is by frying him in this electrical grid? That was one of the great fry-the-alien scenes of all time."

"Marty, I know I'm losing you, but please, please, stay with me for just a little while longer. This next part I'm gonna tell you about could change the course of our planet's history. It is really, *really* important. And I—" She stops suddenly and looks at me. She looks like she could cry, or fly into an uncharacteristic rage, or just go catatonic. "—and I really need your help and support."

I hold her tight and stroke her soft raven hair. "You got my attention, darling. For real. This is pretty deep woo-woo for me, pretty hardcore New Age, but I love you and I am hanging in there. And I know you are not nuts. So please go ahead with your story."

"Thanks. Thanks. Okay, next part. I have discovered that there is a group of people who plan to use this invisible, worldwide energy source to take out China."

Silence. "What did you just say? Take out the china? I don't get it."

"I said Take. Out. China. As in destroy a country. As in bring down the largest country in the world. As in disrupt China's national power grid, paralyze everything mechanical, stop the machines, interrupt all communications, bring an entire country to a standstill and to its knees."

"But why? China isn't a bad country. They're our factory and they're our bank. They own most of our huge debt. They supply Wal-Mart. What have they ever done to us?"

"Just in the last few days I've gotten several clippings in my post office box, all sent from a p.o. box in Page Springs, all about China. These clippings are about the poisoned pet food and human food China has sent to the U.S. recently, the bad toothpaste and the toxic children's toys. And about the pollution and massive dust clouds that originate in China and drift across the Pacific to the U.S. and become our foul air. And yesterday I got a note with the clippings that say China is killing the United States and has got to be neutralized."

"*Neutralized?* Just who are these crackpots? And how do they plan to do this? With a nuclear bomb? This is total madness, Leela. I beg of you to drop this business immediately."

"Can't. Not just yet. They plan to do it, by the way, using EMP—electromagnetic pulse. Sort of like the effects of a nuclear bomb, but without the bomb. And I can't just drop out. I have talked to their people and they want to meet me."

"Wha-a-a-t? *Meet* you? Of course you told them no. Right?"

"Listen, Marty, I need you to get in touch with Hacker for me. Tell him I need a wire, like a mini-minicam with a transmitter. And tell him to study up on EMP. He should also know something about Wi-Fi. And vortexes and ley lines."

"I suppose you want him to pack you a lunch too. Just where is this meeting and when are you going? I've changed my mind. You *must* be cuckoo."

"The meeting is this weekend. It's somewhere in Page Springs in the forest behind the Fish Hatchery. And I *am* going out there. Alone."

I sigh deeply. Whatever Leela wants, Leela gets. It is the very nature of things.

CHAPTER SIXTEEN

A Feeling of Impending Doom

Sedona
2006

January 1, 2006—*The empire, ruled by war-hungry madmen, continues to implode. Nothing is achieved in the house of lords. Corruption, hypocrisy stain the land. Liars lie and thieves raid the treasury. Across the seas, the battles rage. At home, new gurus, some false, some true, are born. The people pray and meditate. False secrets are bought and sold. Reality emerges.*

Sometimes I need to ask Leela what the hell she is talking about in her annual New Year's predictions. Sometimes she tells me, sometimes not. What I get from her is that my website, SedonaConfidential.com, is becoming increasingly important in an age of media lies, half-truths and cover-ups. Watch your step, she counsels; there are wicked men and jealous women out there who could, in her words, "cut your balls off."

Leela is becoming ever more successful as a psychic,

seeing her private clients, conducting weekend seminars at the Creative Life Center, and sometimes doing personal appearances in places like Phoenix, Vegas and Santa Fe. The woman knows how to draw a crowd. She is funny and fast on her feet. I saw her once at a Good Morning Sedona event, and she dazzled the audience with her parlor tricks, her hilarious takes on Sedona and its foibles, and her cheery personality.

It was during one of her out-of-town trips that I first met Alexis Adelstein aka Aura Eaglefeather. At the time she was a waitress at the Sagebrush Café in Uptown, and also a part-time psychic at the Crystal Palace where Leela had her headquarters. She knew Leela, and had seen me with her, so when I walked into the Sagebrush one late night with Hacker she recognized me immediately and came dancing over to our table.

"How are youuuuuuu!" she sang, as she placed the menus on the table, exposing a generous view of cleavage. Aura was a big girl, about 5-5, not chunky but she could have lost 10 to 12 pounds without missing it.

She had a beautiful round face dotted with freckles and framed with a huge shock of red hair—my weakness, I'll admit it—that flowed around her shoulders. And, probably her most outstanding feature, a set of headlights that could wake up a dead man. They looked solid and firm through her flimsy, partially unbuttoned waitress blouse. Hard nipples strained against the tight cloth.

"How's Leela?" she asked coquettishly, balancing on one foot. I knew that she used to be in Leela's Tai Chi class. "I hear she's in Vegas for some sort of convention. Is she behaving herself, do you think?"

It was a setup question, passed off as small talk but

also containing a hint of an invitation. After Aura took our order, Hacker looked at me hard, said, "Dude, that chick's trouble. I may not be psychic, but I can tell you that there's trouble ahead if you mess with that."

I knew that Aura was an avid photographer and spent her spare time photographing UFOs—yeah, right— and little flashes of light that she claimed were conscious orbs from other dimensions. She was real New Age, always talking to her spirit guides and angels and astral traveling to other dimensions and connecting with Source.

Some of her photos had been published in magazines and books devoted to, and read by, the daffy and the delusional. She claimed to have been twice abducted by aliens, teleported to the mothership, and anally probed. There was no proof of this.

When she came around to collect for the check, she asked me if I had ever seen her photographs and if maybe sometime I would like to look through her scrapbooks. I nodded numbly. When she waltzed away from the table, I realized I had left her a huge tip—about 50 percent of the tab. Hacker just looked at me, grinned, and shook his head.

Meanwhile, while Leela was bringing in more and more dough to our family coffers, my website was also beginning to help our cash flow. I hired a local lady to sell advertising, and she was starting to score some big accounts.

My team of Citizen Journalists was beginning to e-mail me some great videos of happenings around town. This became a hugely popular feature on the site, especially such ravers as "Most Embarrassing City Council Moments" and "Best DUI Arrests After Midnight."

I also began a weekly series of articles on the hot-button immigration issue, with a focus on the illegal migrants who flooded Sedona and provided cheap labor. Some of these stories got a lot of feedback.

WHAT IS AFFORDABLE HOUSING IN SEDONA?

Twelve or more illegal aliens stuffed into a single-wide trailer in West Sedona

LET'S GET REAL ABOUT OUR UNDOCUMENTED WORKFORCE

Resorts, shops, contractors, and restaurants love paying the low wages to an available labor pool...but those wages mainly go back to Mexico

After these stories ran, I was accused of being a bigot, a racist, a hate-monger, and Sedona's version of Lou Dobbs. I also got more hate e-mails, threats on my life, and spam attacks. An amateur hacker from Juarez tried to install virulent worms on my server.

Nothing could stop me. By my side I had John Hack, the brilliant computer scientist. He was able to repel any attack on the website. This was in addition to his regular gig of creating websites for clients, his video game development projects, and his favorite hobby: womanizing.

As for me, I was riding high, having fun, making money, and tweaking the status quo as often as possible. I didn't always believe the crap I wrote, but it helped to bring some issues out into the open.

Still...I couldn't escape a feeling of impending doom. I knew some weird shit was about to come down in the very near future. I had no idea what it was. I figured it wasn't really about the website and the shitstorm it was stirring up. No. I could handle any blowback from that. It was really about Leela. And that's what worried me.

CHAPTER SEVENTEEN

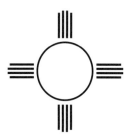

Harnessing the E-Bomb

Sedona
Present Day

It is late afternoon and Leela, Hacker and I are having a serious meeting on our front porch. Jill has come over with Hacker, but she is uninvolved in the high drama at this point and watches TV in the den.

"Lemme get this straight," says Hacker to Leela. "Marty ran it down to me, but I figured him or you must have a glitch in your software." Leela smiles thinly.

"So these guys out in Page Springs are going to bring down China by using an electromagnetic pulse, which by the way is usually caused by a nuclear bomb explosion. Except there won't be a nuclear explosion, right? They'll be using vortex power and ley lines? Did I get that right?"

Leela takes a deep breath and fixes him with her twin green rays. "That's right. And there's more. These people are not just some local crackpot organization from Page Springs or Cornville. They are part of a secret society, something like the Illuminati and the Freemasons. They are all over the world. They are well organized and run by rogue scientists and engineers and financed by bankers and billionaires. They are also extremely serious about this. Their idea is to save the last superpower for capitalism."

"And just how do they intend to harness the awesome power of the world's vortexes, assuming that is even possible?"

"It *is* possible. For one thing, I accessed a lot of this information when I was in the portal. The vortexes are tremendously powerful generating stations, some more powerful than others. When they are linked together via the ley lines, they can produce enough wattage to generate a brief but powerful electronic shockwave that will paralyze anything electrical or mechanical.

"In a fraction of a second, all of China will be brought to its knees and set back at least 200 years. That's what these guys told me on the phone."

Hacker nods his head knowingly. "I've heard of this pulse, this EMP thing. It's called an E-bomb. The U.S. government has been all over this for years. The research is very secret. The Pentagon has been testing their own E-bomb since 9/11. Now they're afraid Iran is going to hit us with an E-bomb—but using a nuclear weapon, not the energy vortexes!" He says this with more than a hint of sarcasm and irony.

Leela moves her chair closer to Hacker's until they are almost nose to nose. "Hacker, darling, this is not a joke. These guys told me they have already wired the major vortexes between here and Asia by probing deep in the earth with some kind of microwave device. They are already online with energy transmissions using the ley lines as electrical cables."

"Fine, fine," says the Hacker, leaning ever more forward and becoming more agitated. "But how do they send the signal?"

"By using the same principle as Wi-Fi—you know, using the FM radio band to send the signal. They reserved a worldwide FM band years ago under the name of some NGO that helps starving people in Africa or something."

"Leela, Leela, Leela!" says the Hacker disparagingly. "You believe this bullshit? It would take gazillions of terabytes of processing power to make all this possible. Where would anybody get access to that much computer power?"

"Try central Oregon," says Leela calmly. "In the middle of nowhere, near a town called The Dalles, near the former Rancho Rajneesh, that commune that got the rednecks all upset a few years ago. Google's server farm is there, covering dozens of acres. Right now Google owns several *peta*bytes of memory and incredible processing power. These guys in the secret society are confident they can hack some of that power, if only for a nanosecond. That would be enough to shut down China."

"Hack Google? Are you kidding? That's like hacking God. You can't hack Google. They've got watchdogs, they've got electronic pit bulls at the gates, they've got firewalls that could repel a hissy fit from Bill Gates. These secret society guys, whoever they are, whatever drugs they're on, are psychos. Get out now, Leela. They are very dangerous."

"They are confident they can hack Google. They are sure they can carry this out. And they want me to help them. They heard about my experiments with remote viewing and they want me to monitor and guide the EMP transmissions."

"Wait a minute," says the Hacker. "Hold on just a goshdarned minute. How do you know about the Google thing? Did these guys tell you that they plan to hack Google? There's a missing piece here, Leela."

"Okay, Hacker, I'll be honest with you. When I was in the portal, I learned how to access hidden information— lots of it. Information is energy, and vice versa. Hmmm, this is difficult. Let's just say I might have read about their plan in the Akashic Records, as if it had already happened. Although it hadn't happened yet. But I saw it plain as day in the Quantum Hologram. Uh—"

"Leela....Where is this going?"

"Hacker, can we cut to the chase? Time is short. Somehow, in some way, I knew about their Google scheme when these people called me up. They admitted it; they didn't try to deny it. Any of it. Look, I have to go meet them tomorrow. If I don't, they have threatened to link the Sedona vortexes and fry all the computers in the Verde Valley, just to prove they can do it. I can't risk that."

I have been sitting quietly, listening, but I can't handle this conversation any longer. It is too weird, way too out there for me, and the whole crazy scheme just might be possible. Leela buys it 100 percent.

I go to join Jill in the den, where she is watching women's tennis. The U.S. Open, no less. The Williams sisters, Venus and Serena, are kicking ass again. They will probably play each other in the finals, again. This makes a lot more sense than EMPs and server farms and rednecks in Oregon.

An hour later I join the meeting on the front porch. Hacker is demonstrating the tiny minicam with transmitter

114

that Leela will wear on her blouse. It looks like a button on the outside; inside her bra is the camera works and transmitter. The plan is that Hacker and I and Jill will monitor her meeting on a huge TV monitor in my office. I offer to follow her to the meeting in my car, but Leela says no. She says the secret society guys have warned her against that.

Leela is going to the meeting tomorrow. Alone. Nothing I can say or do will make her change her mind. This really sucks.

CHAPTER EIGHTEEN

The Unwelcome Wagon
Rolls into Town

Sedona
2007

January 1, 2007—*Immigrants pour into the red city from south of the border to drink from the land of milk and honey, to feast on the ready work and cheap housing. This happens everywhere in the divided empire, where hypocrisy rules. Vigilantes, lawmen with clubs and electricity lash out at the visitors. A great wall is built. Worldwide, a strange ripple in the quantum field. Men of wealth and power seek to take down the Ancient Kingdom. My beloved stirs uneasily under the serpent's shadow.*

I made a conscious decision to throw caution to the winds as the New Year began for me, my wife, and our little entourage in Sedona, Arizona. SedonaConfidential.com tackled some major stories, including government corruption: "EPA Official Once Took Money from Sedona Developer;" local issues: "Real Reason for Demise of Cultural Park I: Booze;" and scandal: "Top Lady Attorney

Admits She Was Once a Man."

In March, I instructed Benny Bravo, my homey and ace reporter, to finalize his story on our big exposé of the day. It ran on April 1. Some people thought it was a joke. The local business people who were involved knew it was no joke.

EXCLUSIVE

SYNDICATE TRANSPORTS ILLEGAL IMMIGRANTS FROM CITY TO CITY

Sedona major hub for Mexican coyote operation; workers packed like cattle into large trucks while government officials look the other way

All hell broke loose after we posted the story. Our office was flooded with e-mails, letters and phone calls. Much of the feedback applauded the story. There was some hate mail. There were a couple of threats on Benny's life as well as mine. Nevertheless, we kept plugging away on the story.

In late May, we posted a follow-up which named names, places and dates. We learned that many businesses in the Verde Valley were deeply involved in the syndicate. We also suspected that organized crime in Mexico was behind it. Some local wags called the syndicate the Unwelcome Wagon. The *Arizona Republic* picked up the story and it went nationwide. Investigations were launched.

In June the dead rattlesnake materialized in my home mailbox. It was the hottest June on record. Even the vibe in Sedona felt freaky and often menacing. When I looked in people's eyes I saw fear and anxiety. Sometimes this is a common pre-Monsoon condition, comparable on some level to PMS, but this felt different.

Adding to my own personal angst was this: After my brief fling with Aura, Leela and I started getting hang-up phone calls at home. At first I thought it had something to do with our exposé of the Unwelcome Wagon. Our Caller I.D. repeatedly said "number restricted." Once when I picked up the phone on the first ring, a female voice said simply "Marty" in a throaty whisper. I knew it was Aura. My blood froze.

There would be no turning back now.

CHAPTER NINETEEN

The Albert Watkins Society

Sedona
Present Day

The flat screen 42-inch TV monitor is up and running in my office, capturing the words and movements of my beloved wife as she drives to her rendezvous with unknown forces in Page Springs, Arizona. It is 1:30 in the afternoon. The minicam and transmitter that Hacker installed in her blouse and bra are working perfectly. The picture is clear and not a bit wobbly, thanks to the steadycam chip in the device.

Hacker, Jill and I watch transfixed as Leela guides her Lexus down Highway 89A toward Cottonwood, gets off the freeway at the Page Springs Road exit, and heads on down the road. Soon she passes a cluster of tumble-down mailboxes at an intersection with a rough gravel road.

"That's the road that leads to John McCain's ranch," Leela says. "Never been there in person but visited once on

121

a little remote viewing experiment," she says. "Nice spread. Lots of security. Bet he's hunkered down out there right now, trying to figure out where he went wrong."

She seems to be taking this all so lightly, whereas we three watchers are nervous wrecks. The camera that looks like a button in her blouse provides a great view of the road, so we can see exactly where she is going. The sound quality from the tiny hidden microphone is amazing. A plan is forming in the back of my mind to follow her trail later and move in on the madmen who want so badly to meet her and use her services.

Leela isn't talking much, but we can hear her car stereo playing Bach's Brandenburg Concerto—great road music for an adventure into the unknown. But just how unknown is it for my gifted psychic spouse? During her trip into the portal, she said she accessed all kinds of information. Who knows? Maybe Leela is still tuned into that channel.

Hacker and Jill merely got stoned on their journeys in the portal (or that's as much as they will admit), while I had the trip of a lifetime plus a taste of satori, or mini-enlightenment. And we all got pretty horny in that portal, a great side effect.

"I'm turning here, just past the Fish Hatchery," says Leela. "I didn't even know there was a road here. That's what the directions say, though." She drives up a rutted dirt road that heads into the hills behind the hatchery. The trees along the road are stunted and the vegetation is mainly sagebrush and scrub oak. Page Springs is only seven miles from the red rocks of Sedona, but Page Springs is no Sedona.

"Look, there's a big old house up there, behind that wall and an iron gate," says Jill, eyes locked on the monitor.

We follow Leela from her POV as she gets out of her car, pushes a button on the gate and enters as the gate slides open. She is greeted at the door by a distinguished looking man with a trim white beard, steel-rimmed glasses and wearing a suit. Strange attire for the Arizona summer. Inside is another man, in his 60s, prosperous-looking, also wearing suit and tie.

The first man has a European-style accent, probably Swiss-German. They show Leela into a well-appointed living room, dim lighting, antique furniture, large oil paintings of French gardens and waterfalls and ponds, flowers, trees. Probably by Monet, maybe copies.

"Welcome to our home, Miss Powers," says the second man, old world manners, clean-shaven, very British. "Please sit and perhaps you would like to join us for an afternoon aperitif? Helga!" he orders. "Please bring the refreshments."

A woman enters carrying a tray of drinks. She looks to be in her early fifties, mildly attractive, hair tied back in a bun, dressed in the style of American women in the post-World War II years—white starched blouse, long skirt, high heels. Leela is quite a contrast in her golden sleeveless blouse and tight Levi's.

Hacker giggles. "Helga? She's quite a winner too. Who the hell are these jokers? They think they're going to take out *China*? They couldn't take out my garbage!"

"Too bad your transmitter isn't two-way," I say. "I'd tell Leela to get her ass out of there and call 911."

"Shhhhh!" scolds Jill. "Let's listen to what they're saying. And what is in those drinks?"

We hear Leela asking the same question. "What kind of drink is this?"

"It's called absinthe, the drink of the gods—and goddesses. It is our elixir. It is the drink of the intellectual elite, the creative geniuses of this world," says the bearded Swiss.

"I think I'll pass," says Leela. "Besides, I don't drink alcohol. Got any Diet Pepsi? Wheatgrass juice, perhaps?"

The second man breaks in. "Absinthe was the drink of choice of Van Gogh, Hemingway, Oscar Wilde, Toulouse- Lautrec, Rimbaud. Geniuses all. It makes you smarter."

"Didn't all those guys go mad?" asks Leela.

Silence, as the three hosts ignore her question, take the absinthe glasses in hand, do a "chin-chin" toast, and down the liquid quickly.

"Look, folks, I'll get right to the point here," snaps Leela. "I've got a very busy schedule. You say you want me to help you—what, destroy China? Because they are evil or something? How can I help, anyway? Plus your scheme sounds pretty far-fetched."

"Your wife has a set of balls, chief," chuckles Hacker, watching the bizarre scene unfolding on the monitor.

The bearded man pulls out a copy of the *Wall Street Journal*. "Listen to this, Miss Powers. 'Huge dust plumes from China cause changes in climate.' It seems all the poison smog from China combined with dust particles blows across the Pacific Ocean on the prevailing winds and changes the climate of California."

"He says that word like Ahnold: 'Kelifornya,'" points out Hacker. "Another freakin Kraut trying to take over the world."

"Who, Ahnold?" I ask. "No, this clown with the beard and the suit," says John Hack.

"Shhhhhh!" begs Jill. "Let's listen to this, please, guys!"

The man rambles on: poison toothpaste, pet food and human food; toxic toys; killer air. All this is second-hand news to Leela, who had been deluged with clippings about China days before. Still, she seems to sit attentively, moving slowly from speaker to speaker so her camera can pick up details of their faces. In my office, Jill and Hacker pay close attention.

"…Not only that," continues the Englishman, "but China is killing the whole planet with pollution. Their economy is growing so fast that it is exploding all over the rest of us. One thousand new cars on the road *every day*. Old-fashioned coal-fired plants dating back to Chairman Mao. The worst, most poisonous air you can imagine. And next, the Summer Olympics in Beijing. That can't be allowed to take place. They must be stopped, Miss Powers. And only we can stop them."

"Just who *are* you people?" asks Leela, a perfectly good question. "And what makes you think your scheme will work?"

"I am terribly sorry," says the bearded one. "We rudely forgot to introduce ourselves. My name is Peter. I am the chairman of our Western branch. And this is Gordon, my associate. And I believe you know who Helga is. Somehow, you know who we are and what we plan to do. We recognize that you are a famous psychic and that you have access to otherwise secret information."

"O-kay," says Leela, stretching out the word. "And…?"

"We belong to a top-secret worldwide organization known as the Albert Watkins Society, named after the English archaeologist who re-discovered the ley lines of the world in 1920. You probably know that we have the means to achieve our goal, and that it is absolutely necessary if the planet is to survive."

"But won't this kill millions of people? How can you shut down China's power grid and all its vehicles and machines and communications and not kill innocent civilians—people just trying to live their lives?"

"Miss Powers," says Gordon solicitously, "are you aware of the principles of Fung Shui? Do you not know where it originated? China, of course. All of China—the whole huge behemoth, the cities, the mountains, the deserts—is all laid out according to Fung Shui principles. We will use these straight, artificial ley lines to send our signal. It will be like a lightning strike. Like a surge that blows out the power in your home.

"Poof! and it's all over for China. Turn the clock back 200 years. Maybe a few citizens wearing pacemakers will be affected, and will suddenly expire, but they were living on borrowed time anyway, so to speak. So there you are."

"Excuse me, gentlemen," says Leela, sounding so calm and composed in the middle of this doomsday scenario, "but where will you get the vortex power for China? The country is so full of negative energy that I don't see how—"

"There are many, many vortexes in China," says Peter, stroking his beard. "Have you heard of the Chinese mystic and philosopher Lao Tzu, the founder of Taoism? He said the Tao is The Way, the cosmic law that directs the unfolding of everything in the universe. And chi, the breath of life, is the wind that comes from the whirling vortex of Tao.

"Miss Powers, China is an ancient land. There are

126

many, many power spots in China, sacred places that the wise ones call vortexes and the bureaucrats call sacred sites for tourists. We have already 'wired' these vortexes with our microwave beams. They are ready to go. The whole system is now online and ready to be engaged. Now all we need is you, Miss Powers."

"Why me? What can I do?"

"We know of your success with remote viewing," says Gordon. "We need someone who can guide and monitor our connections to make sure there are no leaks. A leak anywhere along the ley line system of electrical 'cables,' so to speak, say in Glastonbury or Russia or anywhere, is potentially fatal to millions of innocents. We certainly don't want that. We also need you to make sure the electromagnetic pulse, the EMP, strikes only China."

"Jesus H. Christ," sighs the Hacker, gazing at the monitor, slumped down in his chair.

"This is huge," I add, "friggin huge. Global and really dangerous."

"You do understand," continues the Englishman, "that we are unleashing tremendous power with the vortexes. A power that has never been harnessed in human history. A power that makes the atomic bomb look like a firecracker. So your role is very important to our plan. When you detect a leak or any kind of weakness along the system, you will press a button and the plan will be aborted—temporarily, until the system can be repaired."

"And Google? I'm just curious. How will you hack Google and when?"

"Google's server farm in central Oregon has already been 'hacked,' Miss Powers," says Peter. "They just don't realize it yet. A push of a button and we have all of their processing power, if just for an instant. You must understand, we have the best computer scientists on the planet on our payroll. We have the best scientific brains among our membership. We have unlimited funds and infinite knowledge. The only missing piece is you."

Leela falls into silence as she takes in this information. Her hidden camera catches Helga as she enters the room, whispers something in Peter's ear. He stands up abruptly.

"Miss Powers, my assistant informs me that our scanning software has detected the presence of a transmitting device in this room, possibly on your person. Do you mind if Helga performs a body search on you?"

Leela appears to stand up quickly. The picture becomes blurred as she dashes for the door. She turns around in time to see Helga, carrying some kind of cloth in her hand, put the cloth over Leela's face. The camera jerks to a shot of the ceiling as Leela appears to slump to the floor.

We three watchers are horrified by this scenario. "Leela!" I cry out. "Leela! Holy shit, what have they done to her?"

"Probably chloroform, man," says Hacker sadly.

"I don't believe I'm seeing this," says Jill, sobbing softly.

The last image we see is Helga's grim face in extreme closeup; we hear the sound of cloth being rustled, and then the screen goes blank. They have found the hidden camera.

"Damn, damn, damn!" I cry. "I knew this was a freakin mistake! I knew it! We never should have let her go, Hacker!"

"Boss, I agree with you. But whatever Leela wants, Leela gets. You know that, I know that. She must have figured that this could happen. She must have a backup plan, if I know your wife.

"Let's go out to that house and see if they're still there," says Hacker. "I'll dust off my Magnum and take it with us. Let's take a videocam and a remote transmitting rig. We'll do a live feed to CNN if we have to. This is big. This is huge."

I can only sit with my head in my hands, unable to move. Leela. My beloved. My soulmate. This is the absolute pits.

PART III

CHAPTER TWENTY

A Message from Leela

Sedona
Present Day

I am in the process of seriously freaking out. It has been a week since Leela's visit to the weirdos in Page Springs ended badly. Now she has disappeared, with not a word or clue as to her whereabouts.

Here's what happened: After the three members of the Alfred Watkins Society found out she was wearing a wire and a minicam, they disabled the device and sent her into dreamland. Hacker and I got our act together quickly and raced out to the location behind the Fish Hatchery. Jill stayed behind to monitor any potential communications.

Within an hour, Hacker and I were on the scene at the gated house. Leela's car was gone. The place looked totally deserted. The gate was securely locked. As I tried to climb over the gate, Hacker attempted to pick the lock. We must have set off a silent alarm. Within five minutes three

Sheriff's Department patrol cars rolled up and six very ugly sheriffs emerged with drawn service revolvers.

We were arrested and booked at the Yavapai County Jail for breaking and entering, carrying a concealed weapon (John Hack) and assault on a "peace officer" (me, Marty Powers, for exclaiming, "Hey, that's too friggin tight, motherfucker!") as a sheriff affixed my handcuffs. They confiscated all of our video equipment, as well as Hacker's dusty .44 Magnum.

We spent about 90 minutes in the holding cell at Yavapai County, a very grim place. We called Jill and she posted the 10 grand bail apiece. A hearing was scheduled in 30 days. I wondered, what on earth can we tell a judge? We were looking for my wife because we needed to foil a plot by a bunch of crazies who want to destroy the world's largest country to save the planet? It probably wouldn't work.

Meanwhile, I am such a basket case that I lock myself in our house and refuse to come out. All company business is handled by e-mail. The website is humming along without me. I am deep in the Worry Zone regarding my beloved's whereabouts, so twisted and deranged that I take up eating meat again, drinking wine at three in the afternoon, and even considering lighting up a cigarette after being tobacco-free for many years.

Hacker is worried too, but he occupies his mind with video game development projects, with his new website for foot lovers, and searching the Web for any news or information that might help us locate Leela.

As I pace the front deck of our house, waiting for the Monsoon rain to arrive in the late afternoon on Day 9 of Leela's absence, my cell phone is playing its familiar Beethoven's Fifth. It's Jill, and she is breathless.

"Marty, Marty! You're not gonna believe this, but I just got a message from Leela! I'm sure it's her!"

"What, did she call? Send an e-mail? What?"

"No. No. I don't really believe this is happening. Please, come over to the office. Right now. As fast as you can."

I don't argue with Jill. I clean myself up and arrive at the office within 10 minutes, my heart pounding. Jill sits at her desk staring straight ahead, apparently in some kind of trance.

She jerks awake when I burst in. "Marty, I think it's her, no, I *know* it's her. Leela. It's her voice, I'm sure of it."

I look straight into Jill's eyes. They are wild. "Jill, I don't hear any voice. Where is it coming from?"

"It's…it's…inside…my…head. Like she's talking to me, in kind of a loud stage whisper…inside my head!"

Suddenly I get it. "Jill, are you a telepath? The truth. Please."

"No! No! I don't even believe in that stuff! I think I'm going crazy!"

"Jill, take it easy. I think it's Leela at work. I think you are a natural receiver, and she is sending you telepathic messages from wherever she is. I barely believe this stuff myself, but I know that Leela has incredible psychic powers. Now relax and try to tell me what she has been saying."

"I— I wrote it d-down. Lots of it doesn't make sense. Uh, let's see…all right, here goes. 'Safe. OK. Marty. Mountains. Tibet. Suits. Intervention a must. Dangerous mission. Tell Marty.' Then she said some numbers which I couldn't understand. I think she said latitude and longitude, but the numbers were fuzzy. That's it. I'm sorry, Marty. I did the best I could. I was freakin out."

"You did great, Jill. And there could be more. So stay tuned. And be sure to write everything down. Hey, I wonder if this could be a two-way communication!"

"What? You mean I send messages to Leela? Do you think I could?"

"Why not? Telepathic communication is two-way, at least theoretically. Look, please try it. Next time Leela, uh, rings you up, send her a couple of simple messages: Just think real hard on the words, and visualize the message traveling out of your head and traveling a great distance, then into her head. Maybe in a little capsule or something. Okay? Try this:

"*Where are you?* That's it. Say it several times inside your head. No, you better also say, *Marty and Hacker meet you? Time and place.* Will you give it a try? And I think you ought to stay here in the office. Leela probably figures you'll be here and she can lock into your mind faster and easier.

"You know, there is a foldout bed in that little back office and a microwave and a fridge full of food. Also a TV and a DVD player and some movies. Can you do it?"

"Marty, I am scared shitless. I admit it." She pauses, her face changes, she flips her ponytail and breaks into a deep Southern accent. "Ah'm just a li'l ol' divorcee from Nashville all alone in the big New Age city, an' ah am outta mah depth heah. Unnerstan?"

"Jill, now I know you have gone off the deep end. We never shoulda let you into that portal!" She cracks up, I crack up, and we have a long, hearty laugh. We both need it.

I walk over to where Jill is sitting and kiss her on the forehead. She stands up and we have a long hug. "Jill, you are a living treasure. We are so grateful you are with us."

Jill looks at me earnestly. "Marty, why didn't she send the messages to you? I mean, you guys are really, really close."

"I think it's because she knows I am such a hard case. A doubter, a scoffer, a cockeyed realist. She knows if I heard her voice inside my head I would think I was having an LSD flashback or a schizophrenic episode. So you're the one, girl. You with the open heart and the open mind."

Jill collapses into her chair and I pace around the room, trying to form coherent thoughts. "And I really do think that going into the portal enhanced our consciousness in ways we don't even realize yet. Don't you feel that too?"

Jill nods. "Marty, I'm tired. Do you mind if I go in that back office and just rest awhile?"

"Please go get some rest. Now, I've gotta get in touch with the Hacker and get his input on all this. Would you call him for me? No, never mind. I'm going home, and I'll call him on the secure cell phone line. Our land lines could be tapped, our e-mail is probably being hacked, so please use the cells when you call me, okay? And do call when you hear from Leela again!"

Jill grins, waves bye-bye, and heads for the back office. "Jill, please also double lock the front door, okay?"

I head for home in a big hurry. I already know where Hacker is, and it wouldn't have been wise for Jill to call him. Although they don't have a monogamous relationship, there is some loving energy there. And Jill is a sensitive soul.

The Hacker no doubt is with his latest catch from our Soulmates 4 U online dating service—the life coach from Denver who wrote him that she was soon to visit Sedona for a week, is into kinky sex and new adventures, and likes strong, manly men. I told him that she sounds too good to be true and that she is probably a transsexual or something, but Hacker wouldn't care as long as it has pretty feet.

Hacker picks up my call on the first ring. "I'm kinda busy, dude, whazzup?"

I tell him briefly about the message from Leela, explain that we have to organize a plan immediately. He says he will drop what he's doing and be right over. He forgets to click off his cell phone and I hear the following conversation:

"Hey, sweetheart, an emergency has come up and I gotta go. Now. So could you put your clothes on and—"

"But you— we— we were just starting to…" A female voice, whining.

"I know, but this is a national emergency. I told you I'm involved in some top secret stuff, and our proud nation is in grave danger. I gotta split. I'll call a cab and have them take you back to your timeshare, 'kay?" He realizes that his cell is still live, whispers into it, "Fuck you, Powers," and CLICK!

Less than a minute later the land line rings. A deep male voice. Alarms go off in my internal radar system. His name is Brian Anderson, he is with the U.S. State Department, and he wants to speak to Mrs. Powers.

"She's not available right now. I'll have her call you when she gets back. May I tell her what this is about?"

"This is an emergency situation, Mr. Powers. Her husband, right? I'm sure you understand. This is a matter of national security. I can't discuss it now. When will she be home, sir?"

"I have no idea."

"Mr. Powers, I'm afraid I must ask you to remain in

your home until she arrives. I am sending two agents in an unmarked car to be stationed in front of your home so that we can engage her services immediately upon her arrival. This is a very urgent matter. Please cooperate."

"You can count on me, Mr. Anderson. Uh, where are you sending the car from?"

"Flagstaff. From the Federal Government building here."

"Yes, sir. I'll be waiting." I hang up. I figure I've got half an hour, tops.

Hacker arrives in 10 minutes. By the time he shows up I have secured the house and packed a small suitcase. My personal computer is locked up. We have no incriminating documents in the house. I have no illegal drugs. Let the muthafuggers break in and rummage around.

Hacker is breathless and still buttoning up his shirt when he rushes through the front door. "Hey," he says. "So you heard from the little lady, huh? How's she doin?"

I grab the secure cell, scrape up several $100 bills from the safe, and turn on a bunch of lights. "Hacker, my man," I say calmly, pulling on my Phoenix Suns cap, "we have a problem. Let's get the fuck out of here."

139

CHAPTER TWENTY-ONE

The Mountain Where Shiva Lived

Sedona/Oak Creek Canyon
Present Day

Hacker and I are holed up in his little Oak Creek Canyon hideaway, a rustic cabin facing the dark side of the moon, just about two miles up from Slide Rock. The cabin is a safe house. We decided to plot our next moves here instead of at his home in West Sedona; we figured the Feds would get wise in a few hours and track us to his pad.

Jill calls on the secure cell phone. Great news: She sent my messages telepathically to Leela—Where are you? When should we come get you?—on her own, without waiting for Leela to ring up first. It worked! She got an answer right away:

"Leela said she is on Mt. Kailash. Where is that?" asks Jill. "She also said, 'Don't try to come. Impossible to get here.' I wrote all this down," says Jill. "It was much clearer this time. Then Leela said, 'Cold here, very very cold.' Then she just said in a cheerful kind of voice—you know Leela, Miss Cheerful—she just said 'bye-bye.' And that's it. Now what do we do?"

I am totally thrilled by this news. Thrilled—and mystified. "Hacker and I are going to do some research and get back to you later, Jill. Why don't you get some sleep? It's after 10. Did you eat anything? Maybe you should turn the lights out. Don't unlock the doors for anyone, okay?"

"Okay," Jill says. "I'm kinda scared. But you know I'm a brave girl. Give my love to the Hacker. Good night."

Immediately I open Hacker's laptop and do a Google search on Mt. Kailash. Hacker sits nearby in a big easy chair, chugging a brewski.

"Hey, man, get this. Mt. Kailash is one heavy-duty mutha. It's in Tibet, way on the western side, almost in Pakistan. It is a very holy place! It's friggin remote! It's friggin freezing! And you can't get there by plane, train, or automobile—maybe by bullock cart, and that takes forever. Hardly anybody goes there."

"Then tell me, my captain, what is your ever-lovin wife doing there?" asks the Hacker.

"She needs her space for awhile? I don't know, asshole, what she is doing there!" I snarl at my best friend. "These freakos in the clown outfits probably dropped her there in a helicopter or something. It's got to be tied in with their China scam. Listen to this:

"'The ancient religions spoke of Mt. Kailash as the birthplace of the whole world,'" I read from the Web. "It was a legend before your grandma had her first reincarnation, Hacker. Hindus say the mountain was where Shiva lived, where he did yoga and smoked ganja and sucked it to his lady, the lovely Parvati, all day long."

142

"My kind of god," says Hacker. "Go on."

"There are all kinds of legends around this mountain. One is that the Buddha himself hung out there. It doesn't say how he got up to the top, 22,000 feet. There are all kinds of secrets around this place. Some say it's the key to enlightenment. It is old, very old, and very cold on the summit. And my wife seems to be up there right now. Why?"

The Hacker nods sagely and peers over my shoulder at the computer monitor. "One word, fearless leader. No, make that two words. Energy vortex. This must be one of the heaviest energy vortexes on the planet. That's why these creeps put her up there: to supervise and monitor their crazy frickin scheme to send China back to the Stone Age. You know, to make sure their EMP doesn't take out about half a billion people accidentally. You heard what those jokers said back in Page Springs before Leela went nighty-night."

"I remember the scene well," I note sadly, shaking my head. "But Leela always was a take-charge kind of gal. She'll do her job and do it well. And undoubtedly do something to fuck up their sad-ass scheme."

"Right," agrees my friend. "And I hope she's warm enough up there. She was wearing Sedona summer clothes when she, uh, you know, when she disappeared."

I need to change the subject, so I turn back to the computer screen. "You will notice, my dear Hacker, that Tibet happens to be part of China now. Look at this map. It's official, with no asterisk. No more nation of Tibet. It's been absorbed by the bigger fish. I guess the fight is over. I guess I can put my 'Save Tibet' T-shirts on E-Bay."

"Look, Marty, we need a plan. Or some options

143

when Leela rings us up again. It's her call. Come to think of it, we don't have any options until she hands 'em to us. This is really her show."

"Okay, so let's catch us some zzzzzzz's. I love going to sleep to the sound of Oak Creek. Toss me a brewski, eh?"

CHAPTER TWENTY-TWO

Operation Vortex

Sedona
Present Day

My cell is ringing furiously and jerks me out of a sound sleep. I am on the Hacker's comfy couch. It is just 7 a.m. Jill is on the phone, barely making sense.

"It was her! It was Leela! Clear as a bell! She said we should gather at this place out by the Enchantment Resort. She said you would know where it is. The Mystic Vortex or something."

I get Jill calmed down. We arrange to meet her in an hour at the spot off Boynton Canyon Road that Leela is referring to, a place some people call the Fifth Vortex or the Unknown Vortex or, yes, the Mystic Vortex. This place was known to only a few shamen and some local Jeep tour drivers, including myself, until a couple of travel writers spilled the beans. Still, this supposed power spot is located in a little valley where no one would ordinarily go.

We drive up in Hacker's Prius and are just parking at the trailhead when Jill pulls up in her ancient Volvo. There is space for only two cars. The morning is cloudy and rain is in the air, again. We have a group hug, then set out through a silent forest of juniper, manzanita and piñon pine. Jill's eyes are teary, but joyful. I tingle with anticipation. Jill still hasn't told us why we are here.

Nearly a mile in, there is a little path that leads to a small atoll known as Mystic Vista. This is it. The energy is palpable. We all spin around, arms akimbo, like mad Sufi dancers. There is a 360 view which includes Bear Mountain, Doe Mesa, and the back side of Thunder Mountain with its progeny, Lizard Head Rock.

If you keep turning and aren't falling-down dizzy by now, off in the distance you see Bell Rock and Cathedral Rock—two major vortex sites. Almost in our faces are the fabled red rocks of Boynton Canyon, site of another powerful vortex. Sedona supposedly has four major vortexes, and the only one missing from our view now is Airport Mesa, which is obscured by the towering Thunder Mountain. We are standing at the fifth energy vortex, Mystic Vista.

Jill tells us that Leela has sent specific instructions: We are to sit in silent meditation at a certain spot near a certain ancient juniper tree. Hacker and I are to face Jill, who is to be facing west. We are to empty our minds, if possible, and to simply watch the stream of thoughts that pass by. And wait.

Five minutes pass. Ten minutes. My mind is unusually quiet. The air, the atmosphere is thick and has a strange, almost electrical feeling. I hear a distant, ethereal voice. It almost sounds like Leela.

I open my eyes. Jill's mouth is moving. She sits like

the Buddha. "Beloveds," she says. "It is I. Leela. Jill is my medium now. I am safe. I am on the mountain top, in a warm yurt, waiting for instructions from the men in suits."

I gasp and look at Hacker. He looks at me, his jaw at half mast. We both get it: Jill is channeling Leela! Friggin incredible!

"They will carry out their plan," Jill/Leela continues, "to destroy China. They have stationed me here at a powerful vortex so that I may monitor the energy transmission. They are using the sacred mountains of ancient China, the shrines of Lao Tzu and Chuang Tzu, all of the energy vortexes and power spots in this huge country to transmit the EMP to Beijing and Shanghai and all of the big cities and little villages and even to Lhasa and the rest of Tibet.

"Their plan could work. Everything is online and ready, even Google's server farm in Oregon is engaged. Take a deep breath and close your eyes, beloveds."

It is a Zen moment, timeless, stretching to the far horizons of inner vision. Nothingness. A deep, profound silence. Not even a ripple on the lake of consciousness. Waiting for the next transmission from far off Tibet.

Finally, the ethereal voice continues. "Their headquarters are in Glastonbury. It is an extremely powerful place, in England, near a convergence of many, many ley lines. They will trigger the process from there. The EMP current will have to pass through the ley lines of Europe and Turkey and the whole Middle East where there are some extremely powerful vortexes—in Iran, in Iraq, in Israel—to get to China.

"They have the whole planet wired: Ayres Rock in Australia, Mt. Fuji in Japan, Hawaii Big Island, Mt. Shasta,

Sedona especially—with all the current feeding through Glastonbury. They expect me to use psychokinesis to make repairs and adjustments if there are any problems. The whole process will take just a fraction of a second. I'm not sure what will happen. It is very, very dangerous."

Silence. I open my eyes and look at Jill. This is pretty heavy stuff, and she seems very fragile right now. She is breathing deeply, eyes closed.

Leela again, through Jill: "The operation begins exactly 24 hours from now. Your instructions are to go to a safe place and wait to hear from me. Keep your eyes on the TV news for reports of some strange weather phenomena in Asia, but also here is a website. Stay with it for the real story."

She gives the address of the website twice so we will remember it. And a password. It's a dot-*mil*, which means it's a military site owned by the U.S. government. "Click on 'Operation Vortex,'" she says. "Well, goodbye, beloveds. I send you love from Mt. Kailash at the top of the world. Wish me luck!"

I open my eyes. Jill has fallen over and lies very still on the slickrock where we have been sitting. I put my ear up to her nose and Hacker checks her heartbeat.

"She's fine, she's just exhausted," I announce. "Let's get back to your cabin fast and wait for something to happen in China. And Jill needs to get some sleep. Amazing lady, eh? Who knew she was a telepath *and* a channeler?"

"I sure didn't," says the Hacker. "I just thought she was real smart and a big loveheart with a great body and pretty feet."

"Let's hit the road, you horndog. I'll take Jill's car and meet you guys at the cabin. I'm as nervous as a tourist

148

at a timeshare presentation. Those federales are probably wondering why Leela never came home last night and why I am not there. They are probably looking for me—us— right now. I don't know what they want, but it can't be good."

"That's a big ten-four, Captain Powers. Look, Jill is stirring. Great. I'll scoop her up and we'll head up the canyon. Watch your back."

"Trust Allah, but tether your camel," I reply, and don't know why. I must be channeling some Sufi master.

CHAPTER TWENTY-THREE

DEFCON 2

Sedona
Present Day

Hacker's cabin feels cozy and safe. It's eight in the evening. He has a fire going in the fireplace. We're in late August, but all the Monsoon rain has cooled things down, and the canyon gets downright chilly. Jill sleeps soundly in the bedroom.

I check my answering machine at home, and there is an urgent-sounding message from Agent Anderson of the State Department. He asks me to call him immediately, regardless of the hour. I call him on the secure cell so he and his people can't do a GPS on me and track me down. Hopefully. These bastards have got everything tapped and hacked and wired these days.

I put the cell on speaker so Hacker can hear the whole conversation. Anderson's voice sounds deep and serious, his sentences clipped and urgent. "Mr. Powers, we now

151

know everything. Your wife. We know approximately where she is located. That she is being held against her will. We have agents in England. They are ready to move in on the terrorists."

"Terrorists?" I gasp. "You mean, like, Arabs?"

"Mr. Powers. You are apparently unaware of what is at stake here. The economy of the entire planet would collapse if their plan succeeds. It would ignite wars. Regional conflicts. North Korea could send missiles into a weakened China. Anything is possible."

"And what about Wal-Mart?" I ask, half-serious.

He ignores the question. "We know you have been in touch with your wife. We have monitored telephone calls from your office. Can you communicate with your wife now, Mr. Powers?"

"Shit." I can't believe the office phones are tapped. Even the secure one. I should have known.

"Excuse me?" asks Anderson.

"No, I cannot communicate with my wife," I state impatiently. "I am waiting for a communication from her. She does not have a cell phone, you know. When I hear from her, I'll give you a jingle."

"Mr. Powers, I will share some very confidential information with you. We have an informer inside the Albert Watkins Society headquarters in England. We know approximately when Operation Vortex is to commence. It must be stopped before it starts. The potential consequences are incomprehensible. We know your wife is the key to its success or failure."

I sigh so loudly that Hacker throws me a quizzical look and writes out the texting code "WTF"—What the Fuck?—on a chalkboard. "Mr. Anderson, Agent Anderson,

152

whatever. When my wife, uh, communicates with us again, I will call you immediately. That's the best I can do."

I hear the dialtone. The asshole has hung up on me. So be it.

"What say we get some sleep, Hacker. We got several hours until the big event. I hope Leela knows what she's doing. One thing she said, through Jill, is that this whole business is very dangerous. I think she meant it will be dangerous for her to sabotage the goddamn thing. That worries the hell out of me."

"Not to worry, good buddy. Your lady definitely knows what she's doing. That trip into the portal seems like it really amped up her psychic mojo. Who knows what she is capable of now?"

"Know what really worries me, Hacker? Sometimes one person in a tight relationship takes a sudden jump, spiritual or emotional or whatever, and leaves the other one way behind, trying to figure out wha hoppen. Is Leela taking quantum leaps here? Am I just too lame for her now? Maybe I should go back into that portal and take another cosmic journey—you know, catch up with her."

"Marty, my man, I know you too well. I figure you just want to take another super-acid trip in there. You know, the best Owsley times about a million. That's how you described it. And maybe you'll learn teleportation while you're at it. Even Einstein thought teleporting might be possible."

"Teleportation? Hacker, I'm gonna teleport myself to your nice couch-bed and move into the sleep dimension for about 12 hours. See you in la-la land!"

TEN HOURS LATER

The sound of running water and the smell of coffee wake me up out of a deep sleep. Hacker is fixing breakfast. Jill is already taking a nude swim in the private little swimming hole just down the hill from Hacker's cabin.

The Hacker and I eat a silent breakfast on his deck. Oak Creek Canyon is one of Mother Nature's wonders, and my friend's cabin gives us incredible sweeping views of red rocks and copper canyons and little waterfalls and towering Ponderosa pines. The air itself is scented with pine and sage and a thousand delicate, unnamed scents.

The day passes slowly. I have already checked out the .mil website several times, and the Operation Vortex link is empty. Some of the other stuff on the site is a real eye-opener, though: new, futuristic weapons systems just being shipped to our military personnel around the world; reports on suspected terrorist activity from Liverpool to Lithuania; and on and on and on. It is scary stuff, disgusting, and nihilistic.

I try to get into a movie on Hacker's DVD player, but my mind keeps going to Leela. There have been no new communications from her since yesterday. Hacker and Jill are having a picnic, or something, by the creek. I decide to join them. We all forgot to bring our swimming suits. The water is cool and wonderful as the Monsoon humidity begins to build.

At three o'clock in the afternoon I go back to the military website. I enter the password and click on Operation Vortex. The page is happening now, full of text that makes no sense to me. Military jargon, orders, who knows what.

"Hacker!" I call down to my friend. "The Vortex page is up and running. I can't make heads or tails of it!"

"Be right there, Marty, keep your eyes on it for me."

I see some familiar letters. "Hey, genius, any idea what DEFCON 2 means? It just came up on the website."

"WHAT!?" roars the Hackman from down by the creek. "Stop the presses! I'll be right there!"

Hacker materializes in seconds, minus clothes, and takes a chair in front of the computer screen. I take a position behind him. He checks the text onscreen and makes a sound like "pheeewww," a long, low whistle.

The Hacker looks up at me and shakes his head. "Marty, you're not gonna believe this. The United States is preparing for war. They have thousands of troops massed in Mongolia right now. Right on the China border."

"War? Come on, man. My wife is on top of a mystic mountain in Tibet, a bunch of crackpots in suits think they can shut down China with vortex energy, and America is going to war. Again. Against China this time."

"Whoa, Marty, I didn't say *against* China. They are there to *defend* China. Probably to protect American investments. Look at this."

His fingers point to a bunch of letters on his computer screen. "DEFCON 2. It means Defense Readiness Condition of U.S. military forces. It means our troops are locked and loaded and ready for action. DEFCON 1 means bring out the nukes and get ready to push the button. DEFCON 2 is just short of that."

"Holy shit," is all I can manage to say, weakly.

"If I remember correctly," says the Hacker studiously, "DEFCON 2 has only been used once before, and that was during the Cuban Missile Crisis in 1962. Dude, this is pretty serious stuff."

Staring into space is the best response I can manage.

"Here, let me read some of this crap. A lot of it is in code, but get this: 'USCINCCENT'—that means the general in charge of the operation, Major General Fishface or something—'and all components attained DEFCON 2 at oh-nine-hundred August something something at latitude dah dah dah and longitude duh duh. High alert prepare for possible attack Russia, North Korea, other countries, protect Chinese assets.'"

"What's that mean, Hacker?"

"It means our military is prepared to repel an attack on China from Russia or North Korea or Kazakhstan, for chrissake, and is at full readiness. There are 10,000 of our troops hunkered down within spitting distance of the Chinese border, and they are armed and dangerous. Probably nervous as hell and itching to shoot someone, anyone."

"Oh. Is there anything we can do about it? Like chanting om shanti shanti shanti?"

"There is a slim possibility I can hack this military website and change the orders. Get the troops to drop their weapons, march off in several directions, maybe take a little holiday in the Mongolian countryside. To do this I shall have to consult my favorite oracle, wackyhackers.com. It's got passwords, military code, tips on how to pull some funny hacker pranks, and secret links for launching spam attacks. Serious stuff."

"I don't think we have a lot of time, my dear Hacker. Four o'clock is the witching hour and it's a quarter to. Leela is up there somewhere in Tibet and these crazies in England are just about to push a button of their own. I'm still not sure I believe this vortex business, but I'm ready to believe just about anything right now. Can you hurry?"

"Yo, chief, I am already on it. But please evacuate the premises so I can focus. Thank you."

I slink outside and take a little dip in the creek. Jill has slipped into a halter top and shorts and stands a respectable distance from Hacker, silently watching. Precious minutes pass. Suddenly I hear yelling and whooping from inside the cabin. I rush in, and see my two friends dancing and laughing hysterically.

"I did it!" shouts the Hacker.

"He did it!" shouts Jill. "He changed the orders and the troops all left. That's my genius!"

"Kids, it's two minutes of four. Hacker, could you turn on CNN? Something must be happening in China by now. Or not."

BREAKING NEWS: Bizarre Lightning Strikes Hit China

Video: Continuous lightning strikes light up the night sky over Beijing.

Announcer: "A bizarre series of lightning strikes has hit China, from one end of the country to the other. Beijing has been especially hard hit. There have been sporadic power outages across China, but no injuries are reported and the Chinese power grid has suffered only minor damage.

"A U.S. State Department spokesman said he was meeting with Chinese officials to insure that trade agreements between the two countries would continue uninterrupted. In other words, it's business as usual for the U.S. and China."

We all look at each other and start laughing and crying and shrieking and exchanging high-fives.

"She did it!" I bellow joyously. "Leela did it! She

pulled the plug on those freakin suits!"

My secure cell phone is ringing. A familiar voice is on the line. "Hello!" It's Leela. Jesus H. Christ. "How you guys doin?"

I switch on the speakerphone. "Leela! Where are you, anyway? Still on top of the mountain?" Hacker and Jill are yelling at her at the same time. "Leela! Leela! You did it! You fucking did it!" That's Hacker, of course, totally jacked on jubilation.

"Okay, listen," says my beloved psychic wife. "I am in Varanasi. That's right, India. I bought a nice cell phone from a street vendor. Right now I am dipping my toes in the River Ganges. It is very polluted, but I'll take my chances. Listen, I am going to take a little vacation here by the Ganges. This is a very ancient and very holy place and a real power spot. I may take a day trip to Bodh Gaya where the Buddha got enlightened.

"Then, I would love to meet you all at that ashram near Bombay where Marty and I, um, first met. Anybody got their papers in order? You'll need a visa to get into India."

I've got a current passport, and a 10-year visa for India that still has a month to go. Hacker and Jill unfortunately have let their passports expire. I tell this to Leela.

"Okay, Marty, how about you and I meet there in about three days over a chai in the Zorba the Buddha restaurant? I've got a few burns on my arm and leg but don't worry, I'm okay. You other two, I'll see you in Sedona and we'll have a little get-together and gossip at our house."

We three are whooping it up, dancing around and totally crazy with joy. Leela has to shout to be heard above the celebration.

158

"Marty, when you go to our house please also get my passport and bring it with you. I left the USA in a hurry and didn't bring it with me, dearest. And please call that nice Mr. Anderson. He is waiting to arrest those bad men in Glastonbury who are behind this whole crazy business. Bye-bye!"

She did it. My wife. Somehow, she aborted that crazy, dangerous, impossible scheme. But how? And how did she get down from that inaccessible mountain and to Varanasi in just a few minutes? Questions, questions, many questions, and each one just leads to another question.

I pull on my clothes and hold up the keys to Jill's Volvo. She nods in my direction, meaning it's okay to take her car. "I gotta go, team. I'll call you from India. Have a good one!"

CHAPTER TWENTY-FOUR

Where Is the Real Leela?

India/Sedona
Present Day

Leela and I do indeed reunite at the ashram near Bombay. Only now it is called a "meditation resort" and it is even more wonderful, full of life and beautiful people and great, healthy food and lots of activities to raise our consciousness and shake our booties. I am so happy to see her that I nearly squeeze the breath out of her.

"Leela, you've got a lot of 'splaining to do," I say over a gourmet Japanese feast at a cozy little outdoor restaurant in the resort. "For starters, how did you get from the top of a mountain in Tibet to Varanasi in just a few minutes? Sherpas on roller skates?"

She laughs easily, flashing those wild green eyes, those white even teeth, those high-fashion cheekbones. "Let's save that one for a few minutes, okay darling? First let me tell you how I managed to sabotage the whole operation by using a little telekinesis trick I learned in the portal."

"Okay, start with tele— uh, telekiss something."

"You know, telekinesis. TK. Some people call it psychokinesis, or PK. The ability to move objects by using the mind. Edgar Mitchell talks about it. He says it is theoretically possible to move large objects with PK, but he says we still don't know how to do it. He says what's missing is the 'energy transfer mechanism,' I think he called it.

"Well, I figured out the mechanism. I can't even put it into words; maybe I could diagram it for you some day. So anyway I was able to tweak the electrical system the suits had set up and divert the movement of energy just enough so that the whole thing was aborted and just released a bunch of harmless lightning all over China. Couple big bolts just missed me on top of Mt. Kailash."

She shows me the burns up and down her right arm and on her right thigh, raw-looking red blotches. I kiss the ones on her arm, but can't quite reach the ones on her thigh.

"But all this had to happen in about half a nanosecond," I say. "The Google hack must have been working, the vortex current is flowing. How could you do all that so quickly?"

"Simple. I didn't do it in real time. Ever hear of dimensional teleportation? Another little trick I learned in the portal. It means you leave the physical universe at one location and re-enter it at another location.

"In other words, I stepped out of the space/time continuum for maybe a *femtosecond*—that's one-thousandth of a nanosecond—moved my physical body over a few microns, did my work in my own good time, or non-time, then re-entered the physical plane of existence at a different location."

"But L-l-leela," I sputter, trying to follow her. My wife has become a super genius now.

"I was moving between parallel universes," she explained. "No problem. You know, Einstein was fooling with this idea years ago, but died before he could prove his theories. Too bad."

My head is spinning. "Okay, okay. Let me get this straight, sweetheart. You have learned the secrets of psychokinesis and teleportation. Moving between parallel universes. Etc., etc. So please be straight with me: Did you teleport from Mt. Kailash down to Varanasi? And if you did that, aren't you just a copy? Didn't all of your atoms dissemble and then reassemble at the other end?"

I am kind of kidding around, playing with words and old school sci-fi ideas, but I am also very serious. I am also a new believer. Call me neo-New Age. My wife has been messing with some pretty powerful stuff. It obviously works. My ideas of woo-woo have gone bye-bye. Leela must know this.

"Are you the real Leela, or is there another one floating around in cyberspace or something? Is this 'Beam me up Scottie' or Nikolas Tesla? Where is the real Leela? The truth, darling."

"Yes, no, yes, no, yes yes yes—I am the real one! Scottie did not beam me up. I just moved into another dimension and— Sweetheart, I can see the worry lines around your eyes." She stops talking, closes her eyes, takes several deep breaths, and puts her fingers on my third eye. I feel an incredible tingling sensation throughout my whole body.

"Marty, you are my guy no matter what happens in the outer world. I love you as much as ever. You really have stuck by me and supported me even when I acted crazy. You are the smartest, sweetest, funniest man I have ever known. You still turn me on. A lot. Would you get the check now and can we go back to our hotel room? Please."

I move very quickly. I never say no to a woman who says "please." Especially when she says it with that kind of urgency. Especially when it is my beloved wife.

FORTY-EIGHT HOURS LATER - Sedona

The celebration is in full swing on our front deck. The booze is flowing freely (fruit juice for Leela) and live music is happening: Hacker on guitar, me on the Yamaha keyboard, Jill on flute, and Leela on percussion, pots and pans plus wooden spoon. Leela has told Jill and Hacker all the details of how she sabotaged the China caper and both are sworn to secrecy. Nobody outside of our little circle would believe it anyway!

Including Mr. Anderson. He called a few minutes ago and told us that his agents had arrested the head honchos of the Albert Watkins Society in Glastonbury, and they were hot on the trail of other society members. He said the potential worldwide financial and military crises were over. He gave big thanks to Leela for her role in the aborted project, and wanted to know how she had done it.

"Meditation, Mr. Anderson," Leela had said gravely. "Years of meditation. Yoga. Tai chi. The spiritual life. You should try it, Mr. Anderson. It'll give you a whole new outlook." And she hung up.

Now there is only one missing piece, you should pardon the expression: Aura Adelstein. She is out there somewhere, a ticking time bomb, holding a scrap of information that could ruin my marriage and my life.

164

The land line rings. Leela puts down her improvised percussion instruments, checks the caller I.D., and picks up the phone. "Uh huh," she murmurs. "Uh huh. Yeah, okay, yeah, yep. Got it. Okay. I'll check in with you tomorrow. Bye, Aura."

Aura. Damn. Synchronicity, or a Cosmic Joke? "How's she doing?" I ask my wife, trying to appear nonchalant. I discover that I am holding my breath and my guts are churning.

"Strange," says Leela. "She says she is morphing into a higher being. She is not the old Aura or Alexis anymore, she says. She has access to 'higher knowledge' and knows the secrets of the stars? What's up with that?"

The live music has stopped and everyone is listening.

"And she now knows that she wasn't really struck by lightning out there on Bell Rock, but her consciousness was invaded by alien orbs from another dimension. Wow."

"Pathological," says Jill.

"Pathetic," says Hacker, looking sideways at me.

"Supercalifragelistic expialidocious!" says I, exhaling mightily.

"Om shanti shanti, peace on earth, and let the party continue!" says Leela.

CHAPTER TWENTY-FIVE

Karma Crossroads

Sedona
Present Day

> *What a pity!*
> *A person lost at*
> *The crossroads of karma*
> *Though right in the midst of Paradise.*
>
> — *from* A Zen Harvest

Please do not pity me. I was lost, but now I am found. I am also rich. And I live in the midst of Paradise: Sedona, Arizona. I am happily married to a beautiful, intelligent—let's not forget psychic—woman. Life is good, better than I ever thought it could be.

A few months ago, however, I *was* living at the

crossroads of karma, dancing on the precipice, flirting with disaster, and daring the Beast to come and get me. It almost did, but Leela saved my ass. *Our* ass. Let me explain. It was a few weeks after Leela short-circuited the scheme by the Albert Watkins Society to bring down China and save the world for capitalism. I took her success as a sign that we were on a roll. My spirit guides (yeah, right) told me to up the ante with my website and go after some really scandalous and/or illegal behavior. Time to be a big-time whistle-blower, I thought, time to make some national, screaming headlines.

My two ace reporters, Benny Bravo and Cole Warner, had been working on several big stories. Three of our CJs (Citizen Journalists) had sent in some shocking reports on the same stories, and Jill, our ace fact-checker, had found all the details in order.

Jill seemed uncomfortable with the direction we were headed, but didn't say much. Hacker only encouraged me to "go for their throats." Leela was out of town, in New York for a week to do some work for an advertising agency that paid very well for her remote viewing skills. I didn't want to bother my wife with Sedona trivia, namely the nefarious schemes I had up my sleeve, during our nightly phone conversations.

The plan was this: On a Monday, we would publish three teaser headlines and short blurbs promoting the stories we were about to break in Sedona Confidential. The full stories, bombshells all, would run on the following days. The first headline went like this:

OPERATOR OF RED ROCK ESCORT SERVICE BUSTED; CUSTOMER NAMES TO BE PUBLISHED HERE SOON

It was a great story about an FBI sting operation and the lady owner of the service who turned over her phone book to us as a legal defense strategy. The phone book included the names of celebrities, politicians and prominent businessmen.

How could we follow that? The story for day two involved drug busts and narco kingpins in the Verde Valley. We intended to name names and places, and blow the lid off the local drug distribution network.

Day three, and another major scandal: "Developer Plans to Turn National Forest into 'Secret Mountain Estates.'" Seems a Phoenix developer had "convinced" a Federal judge to overturn the law that protects the national forest surrounding Sedona from being developed. The guy planned a billion dollar project for the superrich which would replace the wilderness. We had the goods on both the developer and the judge, a Reagan appointee.

Sunday night, 8 p.m. I sat in the office alone, staring at a computer monitor. Jill and I had just finished inputting the teaser headlines and blurbs for posting on Monday morning. Hacker had set up the data both as text and with animated speaking characters. That meant if you had a fast Internet connection, you could watch and hear a beautiful female robot deliver the headlines and blurbs. Jill had input the voice part.

Jill and Hacker left to have a Japanese dinner in Uptown. I closed my eyes. All that was left was to push

169

ENTER and a series of events would be set in motion, events with unpredictable outcomes. Do I really know what I'm doing? I thought. Of course I do. I am riding high. I am in my power. Marty is in his Powers. Heh heh. Heh heh heh heh!

Sudden thought: Power corrupts. And absolute power corrupts absolutely. Lord Acton said that. Ego corrupts. Ego corrupts and deceives and leads us down dark, dangerous paths. I said that.

I wonder if I really need to do this, said my internal voice. I have already received death threats from all of the stuff we've run on illegal immigrants. The dead rattlesnake in the mailbox. The "looks that could kill" from Latino neighbors. The warning from a friend at the local newspaper to watch my back.

And now, am I once again endangering the lives of my wife, my close friends, my own life? Naw, I thought, this is a public service. I'm just being paranoid. The public needs to know this stuff. My right index finger paused above the ENTER key. One quick motion and…

The telephone rang. Strange. Maybe it's Jill or Hacker. They forgot to tell me something. No, they would call on the cell. "Hello!" Caller I.D. said a hotel in New York City.

"Marty? It's Leela! What are you doing right now?" There was an urgency to her voice, a strident quality that was very un-Leela-like. We had already talked hours earlier, just the gossip of the day. It was after 11 in New York, late for my early bird wife.

"Just sitting here, staring into space, thinking," I answered as nonchalantly as possible. I didn't want to involve her in my business, which she has found distasteful lately.

"Marty, listen to me. I just had a vision that something terrible is going to happen to you. It was like a dream, but it was much more real. It woke me up out of a sound sleep. There is an explosion, a big one, in your office, and a terrible fire, with people running out of the building. The office burns to the ground and everything in it burns to a crisp. The house in front burns too. It is a terrible, terrifying scene."

I took a deep breath and told her everything: my inner conflict over posting the three stories, the warnings, the danger to all of us. She begged me not to post the teaser headlines. She said she felt that I was at a kind of karmic crossroads, that my future—our future—would be either beautiful or disastrous, depending on whether or not I pressed that ENTER key. And would I mind deleting the stories or waiting until she got home so we could discuss it?

When Leela speaks, everyone listens. When Leela says she can see the future and it could get ugly, you don't argue. I told her I would go home and call her in the morning. I told her I would sleep on it, think it over. I already knew what I was going to do.

Next morning I woke up early, 6 a.m., a crisp, clear mid-October morning in Sedona. I rubbed the sleep dust out of my eyes, looked around, and saw that I was indeed at the Karma Crossroads. The decision had already been made for me.

In short order I shut down SedonaConfidential.com; sold Soulmates 4 U to Yahoo for $5 million; spun off Cybersluts as a separate website with a new name, "Cybersluts69," at Hacker's behest; and decided to become an environmentalist.

It didn't matter that everybody and his uncle was

jumping on the environmental bandwagon. It couldn't hurt. My career as a muckraker and whistleblower was over. I called Leela that fateful morning from the Karma Crossroads, and she was back in Sedona that evening.

We had one of the best reunions of our lives. Candles. The proper music. A firm kingsize bed. And the goddess Tantra as our guide.

Afterward, as I drifted off into dreamtime in the arms of my own goddess, I remembered the words of that Indian guru. He said love is a miracle. And that love is alchemy, the most profound science of transformation. Something like that.

Leela stirred sleepily, her body pressed against mine. "Don't forget my favorite line by Emily Dickinson," she purred. "'Love is all there is.'"

That works for me, I thought. Wait a minute—did Leela just read my mind again?

New Goddess in Town

Sedona
Four months later

Hacker and I sprawl indolently in our plush new offices on 89A. All of the legal and technical details of the Soulmates 4 U sale and transfer to Yahoo have been completed, and the money is in the bank. Five million U.S. dollars. Time to share the wealth.

"Hacker, my man, we are rich. Rich, do you hear me?!" I shout, half-mad with money lust as I hand him a check for $2 million. "We are loaded, and I'm talking money here. We are well-heeled, affluent, well off, prosperous, flush with cash. Can you dig it?!" I had already given Jill her check for $1 million. She had come close to fainting.

The Hacker, of course, always stays as calm as a tour guide on a bus full of excited Japanese tourists. "Hey, man, your new site is up on the Web and ready for you. Now, what you gonna do wid it? And what you gonna do for excitement from now on?"

I do a test run of SedonaGoGreen.com. Wheeeee! It is beautiful. Animation, interactive features, artificial intelligence, talking avatars, a video room, chat rooms, blogs, great links to proactive eco-sites, and more, much more.

"Hacker, I have seen the light, and it is green. You see, green is the color of the heart chakra. I have moved from the head to the heart.

"We are in a whole new era. I've done all I can to expose the evils of our society, to reveal for all to see the sordid underbelly of American-style capitalism. The hypocrisy, the lies, the deceptions, the blatant criminal behavior. Now—"

"Uh, dude, I hate to pop your bubble, but what do you intend to do about the, uh, speaking of hypocrisy, the sordid underbelly of your girlfriend Aura? Are you ever going to tell your psychic wife? Or does she already know?"

"You are a lowlife cur, a perverted, foot-lovin pile of steaming dogshit!" I hurl at my best friend. I can say this because he knows I love him. "Of course I will tell Leela! You can take that to the bank! Along with your friggin check for two mil, a-hole!"

It is true, I am beset with guilt re my sorta-sordid affair with Leela's friend Aura. But things have changed.

Rumors are swirling around Sedona that there is a new goddess in town. Her name is Kali. They say she is very charismatic, that she seems surrounded by a magical and inviting energy field. She is starting to attract followers, and is now holding *satsang*—which means, literally, sitting with a guru or teacher—every evening at 6 p.m. in her new luxury home, which was donated by a wealthy follower.

This new goddess is the former Aura aka Alexis

Adelstein. They say she has gained 20 pounds, wears flowing golden robes, and gives discourses on spiritual subjects in a strange, ethereal voice.

Leela and I discuss this phenomenon one evening over dinner at our favorite Thai restaurant. I figure that this is as good a time as any for my confession. The old Aura seems to be gone, almost a figment of the imagination. Leela has been out of touch with her former friend, whom she describes as "an entirely new person."

Leela and I have moved out of our old Andante Drive neighborhood, which has become a kind of make-believe barrio. We have moved to the upper reaches of Mountain Shadows Drive in West Sedona. There, Navajo-style, we live nearly a quarter-mile from our nearest neighbor. And that's the way, that's the way I like it.

Although we now have some money, Leela continues her psychic work. She rarely sees private individual clients, except those who have been with her for years. Her clientele now includes several big corporations, all of whom have some connection to the environmental movement. And lately she has taken on jobs with the U.S. State Department, which require the use of her remote viewing skill set.

"Leela." I look straight into those penetrating green eyes, poking at my tofu pad thai with chopsticks. I have returned to vegetarianism. "Darling, there is something I have to tell you."

"Marty, sweetheart, you seem so serious. What's up? You better tell Mama." My beautiful wife is in a festive mood. It is February and we are in the middle of a very cold winter. Snow is on the ground. She giggles as she loads up her mouth with chicken fried rice.

"Leela." This is the moment of truth, the moment I

have feared for months. "I have— I mean, I did— I mean, I-I-I—"

Leela's cell phone rings. "Hold it right there, Marty, I gotta get this. Yes? Mr. Anderson? What is it? Wha-a-a-t? They plan to— That's hard to believe. So what can I— Okay, the airport, half an hour? Seriously? Okay, got it. Got it. See you at Sky Harbor."

Leela turns slowly to me and pushes her food away. "Marty, you're not gonna believe this, but I gotta go to Washington D.C.—tonight. They've got a helicopter at the Sedona airport waiting for me, and a military jet at Sky Harbor in Phoenix."

"But— but sweetheart, I need to tell you about the—"

"Marty, please leave some money on the table and let's get out of here. I gotta pack and get on the chopper. Right now." Chopsticks in hand, she takes one last stab at her food, fills her mouth with fried rice, and stands up.

"But— but—" I look over her shoulder. Snow is falling again. "Look outside, sweetheart, it's snowing like crazy! How you gonna take a helicopter to Phoenix in this—"

"Marty, I don't have a choice! And you can tell me later what you were gonna tell me. I'll call you in the morning from D.C. Better fasten your seat belt. Here we go again!"

TO BE CONTINUED

Don't miss Book 2:
The Alien Manifesto,
second installment in the
I Married a Psychic trilogy.

Check our website
for up-to-date information:
www.vortex23.com.

Sources

google.com

wikipedia.org

Skeptic's Dictionary
skeptic.com

Edgar Mitchell, "The Quantum Hologram"
edmitchellapollo14.com

Vortexes and ley lines:
ofspiritandsoul.com/
angelfire.com/indie/anna_jones1/vortexes
geo.org/

unitedstatesaction.com/

sacredsites.com

religioustolerance.org/newage.htm

sitepal.com

Osho, "The Razor's Edge," "Guida Spirituale"
osho.com

Gratitudes

Normally, this page in a book would be called "Acknowledgements," and it serves to thank all those who have helped the author in some way. But a deeper look into the word acknowledgements reveals that it is rather shallow, more like a casual nod to someone, a disingenuous thank you, nearly in the same vein as "have a nice day."

I have chosen to use the word gratitudes. It is much more spiritual, more deeply felt, more from the heart. It is an outpouring of thanks, of profound and utter gratefulness.

And so I wish to express my gratitude first to Existence, to the great Cosmic Joker, for allowing this book to happen.

I give the highest praise and deepest thanks to my wife and muse Liberty, and to my cat and muse Maggie for their love and support.

I give praise to the skies and total gratitude to Dr. Nathan Avery of Flagstaff, the brilliant surgeon who performed a successful cervical fusion on my upper spine on 9/5/05, saving my precious fingers from going numb and my limbs from going useless.

Special thanks to my inspirations in Spontaneous Writing: Allen Ginsberg and Jack Kerouac. "First thought, best thought"—the phrase that Ginsberg used to describe spontaneous and fearless writing. Kerouac said, among many things, "Write in recollection and amazement for yourself....Be in love with yr life."

Very special thanks to my writing guru, Natalie Goldberg, teacher, author and poet, whose "Writing Down the Bones" is the bible of Spontaneous Writing, and is rooted in Zen practice. And deepest gratitude to the Sedona

Writers Workshop, which still meets and still practices the principles set forth by Ms. Goldberg.

You have all helped to make this book possible, and I am grateful, amazed, and filled with wonder at how it all comes together!

Marv Lincoln

Multimedia Time Traveler

He began writing professionally at the age of 16, and over the years he has written on nearly every imaginable subject. He has worked as a newspaper reporter, media critic, magazine and book editor, photojournalist, short story creator, and novelist.

His portfolio includes writings on such diverse subjects as computers and software, film, music, art, sports, spirituality, politics, real estate, sexuality, hot rods, finance, medicine, travel, and pop culture.

Marv wrote and sold two James Bond-style novels in the early Seventies He is a playwright and screenwriter, and made several experimental films decades ago. With his wife Liberty, he was co-host of a long-running cable TV show in Los Angeles, "The Cosmic Couple Presents."

During his career, he has interviewed—and written about—many celebrities, including Andy Warhol, Charles Bronson, Sterling Hayden, Sean Young, Robert Shields, Jill Ireland, singer Donovan Leach, Sr., and Gerard Damiano, director of the most profitable film of all time, *Deep Throat*.

Today Marv lives in Sedona with Liberty and with Maggie, their cat since 1996. During his time in Sedona he has worked as a tour guide, restaurant server, DJ, stand-up comic, editor, and feature writer. He now writes extensively for the Internet, and is partners with Liberty in a Sedona public relations firm. They maintain a weblog called "Thunder Mountain Views."

Marv has been a practicing meditator since 1979. He enjoys hiking in Sedona's red rocks, swimming, and hanging out with his wife and pussycat. Now he's a science fiction novelist, which he always wanted to be.

Sedona, Arizona
Autumn 2007